"That's quit   e."

The nurse spoke to Cassie while making a note on her chart.

"Thanks, but Noah's not my man. He's my guardian angel."

And speaking of angels…

The sleeping angel Cassie held in her arms took her breath away. Had there ever been a more beautiful sight?

Emotion swelling, she blinked back tears. Every bit of the anguish she'd been through was worth it. Not only was *she* alive, but she was holding her very much alive baby in her arms, with another perfect baby waiting in line for her breakfast.

And just think, she had this double blessing and her own life all because of Noah. Though the actual delivery of her babies had become a blur, he was the one thing about her ordeal that she'd never forget. His soothing voice, and the way he'd held her hand, urging her not to give up.

Starting at the still-warm spot on her forehead where Sheriff Noah Wheeler had planted his tender kiss, she felt a quiet contentment creep through her.

Dear Reader,

Some of my books contain more of the real me than others, and *Babies and Badges* is definitely one of the stories with a lot of me! First, I grew up in Springdale, Arkansas, which is only about forty-five minutes from the fictional small town of Riverdale. This mountainous part of the state is gorgeous any time of the year, but the story opens in spring, when the leaves are such a luminous shade of green that they look as if they're floating. The smells are heady. Rich and loamy and sweet. Okay, so clearly I love the setting. Ah, but the people of Arkansas I love even more. Lots of quirky true individuals never in such a hurry that they can't take time out to share their day.

The hero of this story, Noah Wheeler, was a football star at the University of Arkansas, where I graduated in 1989. Cassie, the heroine, is an interior designer in Little Rock. While I never practiced there, right out of college I did interior design work for what have since become two of the most prestigious architectural firms in the state. All of that is just backbone to the story. Many of my favorite things wove their way in. The War Eagle Craft Fair. Saturday morning yard sales. Steeple Hill author Margaret Daley's hot yellow Thunderbird convertible...and my love for all deep-fried foods!

For those of you who've never had the pleasure of visiting this enchanting state, I hope reading Noah and Cassie's story will tempt y'all into coming on over for a visit real soon!

Laura Marie Altom

I love hearing from readers at P.O. Box 2074, Tulsa, OK 74101 or by e-mail at BaliPalm@aol.com. And check out my Web site at www.lauramariealtom.com!

BABIES AND BADGES
Laura Marie Altom

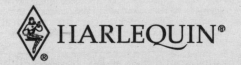

TORONTO • NEW YORK • LONDON
AMSTERDAM • PARIS • SYDNEY • HAMBURG
STOCKHOLM • ATHENS • TOKYO • MILAN • MADRID
PRAGUE • WARSAW • BUDAPEST • AUCKLAND

ISBN 0-373-75032-3

BABIES AND BADGES

www.eHarlequin.com

Printed in U.S.A.

For my dear grandmother-in-law, Wanda Thompson-Davis—better known in the family as Nana—and her husband, Sonny Thompson, whom I'm deeply sorry never to have known. How you two got left off my special grandparents' dedication I'm still trying to figure out! In the meantime, please know how much you mean to all of us here in Tulsa!

Chapter One

Sheriff Noah Wheeler glared at the pink rice bag occupying his passenger seat and muttered, "I'll give you a *Here comes the bride...*"

Tightening his grip on the wheel, telling himself the muggy May breeze ruffling his hair through the ancient Suburban's open window was relaxing instead of annoying, he sighed.

What the hell had he been thinking attending Kelsey's wedding?

Was he some kind of sicko masochist?

He'd given that woman some of the best months of his life—eight to be exact. They'd traveled. Done Branson, Missouri. Taken a fountain tour of Kansas City. No destination had been too much trouble. Shoot, he'd even driven her all the way to Fayetteville on a weeknight just to see Christmas lights on the square! He'd barbecued with her, made grilled cheese sandwiches for her when she'd broken her pinkie finger. He'd changed her car's oil. Driven her to work when she'd gotten that bogus new set of tires.

In short, he'd done everything for her.

And what had she done for him?

Gone off and married another man—one of his good friends, dammit. And then had the gall to invite him to the wedding!

Time for the truth yet, Wheeler? Or you gonna stay hitched to this pity train for the rest of your life?

He glared at the road winding its way through northwest Arkansas. At tender new leaves in the forest thick with maples and oaks and fading redbuds. At tender side-of-the-road grasses just tall enough to sway in his truck's breeze.

By the end of next week, traffic would be bumper to bumper with RVs and minivans heading for the twice-annual War Eagle Craft Fair, but today, at least, the highway was deserted.

Just like him.

And that was how he liked it. He was a bachelor. The best of a dying breed. He was a downright professional single guy who'd long ago decided to be happy with his eternally single state.

Nope, no more moping for him.

Cruising past Judi Thompson's place with her rows of hybrid irises looking like pastel Easter eggs fastened atop fragile green stems, he decided to be happy about spring. Not just spring, the season, but this newfound spring in his life.

His conscience snorted.

Good one, buddy. Mind B.S.ing your way back to the truth?

Noah pressed his lips tighter than the zipper on a virgin's prom dress.

Okay, so maybe if he were honest with himself, he'd admit he was a little blue. And maybe Kelsey had tearfully broken things off with him for a very good reason—at least in her mind. And okay, yeah, her new husband, Owen, had requested Noah's permission before even asking her on a first date. But geez, did he have to go and get hitched to her?

Okay, so maybe Noah *did* have certain issues with even saying the word relationship, let alone m-marriage.

See? He could barely even think it!

But she could've stuck by him.

She could've been content for them to spend the rest of their lives dating. Just like he was. But she'd stubbornly insisted on the two of them tying the knot, going so far as to give him an ultimatum. Either he marry her or it was over. He'd been every bit as bullheaded, insisting they maintain the status quo. They didn't need rings to show the world they were a couple.

Shoot, they'd had matching Razorback T-shirts, and he'd spent Christmas and Thanksgiving with her family instead of his. What more could a woman want?

Judging by today's ceremony—a lot!

By God, Noah Wheeler always—*always*—honored his commitments. If he said he'd stick by her, he would. He just didn't see the need to go making it all official.

He'd already gone that route, and everyone in the county knew darned well what'd happened.

The drive from Eureka Springs's famous Thorncrown Chapel grew more tedious by the mile—or maybe it was Noah's own company getting on his nerves. Whatever the case, he reached into the glove box where he kept an emergency stash of candy bars and pulled out a Twix.

He'd just put the gold foil wrapper to his teeth when he spotted one of those fancy new Thunderbird convertibles with its flashers on a couple hundred yards up the road. The pale-yellow dream on wheels was way too new to be having mechanical problems, so he figured the owner must've run out of gas.

Thrilled to have a distraction, Noah eased his SUV onto the wide shoulder behind it, grateful the car's driver had had the good fortune to not run dry on one of the many sections of the road with a steep drop-off.

Noah had already pulled off the tie he'd worn to the wedding, and after easing out of his truck, nursing his aching left knee—always a barrel of monkeys in this muggy weather—he ditched his jacket as well, tossing it on top of the rice bag he planned on letting the guys down at the station use for target practice.

Without his radio or gun, he felt naked approaching the car. He could've called in his stop on the fixed radio in the truck, but didn't much see the need. Judging by the long, wavy hair, he could tell a woman sat in the front seat, head slumped against the headrest. Probably taking a nap.

"Hello!" he called out, walking slowly toward the driver's side.

When he got no answer, his heart beat faster.

Was she hurt?

"Hello? Sheriff Noah Wheeler here. Just checkin' to see if you need any help."

A VW Bug whizzed by—the old kind.

Red.

The exhaust stung his nose.

Senses on full alert, wondering if maybe he should call in, he crept closer still. "I'd sure appreciate a wave or something. You know, just to let me know you're all right."

Greg Morris down in Washington County had gotten shot approaching a vehicle. The woman driver had played dead, while in the passenger seat her boyfriend hunkered down with a .357 Magnum. They'd been running drugs to the U of A campus from Dallas. Greg was now in a grave, and Noah hoped his killers spent the rest of their lives in the equivalent, only with concrete walls instead of dirt.

His pulse hammered, and a bead of sweat slid down his right temple.

Damn this heat and this stupid dress shirt.

He could see through the rear driver's-side porthole window that the passenger seat was empty. But since he couldn't see if the woman was truly asleep, or hurt, or just playing possum, he took it slow.

"Ma'am? You need help?"

"Mmm…"

He raised his eyebrows. Had that been a moan?

Throwing caution to the wind, heart racing as he prayed this wouldn't turn out like that nightmarish Monday on Blue Springs Road, he finished his approach, and wished he'd done it a lot sooner, as the woman behind the wheel was about twelve months pregnant and obviously in trouble.

Her window was down, so he lightly shook her shoulder. "Ma'am? Can you look at me?"

Resting on a pillow of her lush red hair, she inched her head to the left, then opened exotic jade-green eyes a millimeter at a time. "I—" She licked her lips. Full, kissable lips attached to a flawless complexion—which must've cost an awful lot of money to keep up. The kind of money that had no business being on the side of the road in desolate Pritchett County. A fine mist of sweat coated her forehead and upper lip, and her breathing was erratic. She licked those lips of hers again, then said, "I—could you please help?"

Her gaze fell to her bulging tummy.

His gaze followed. "You in labor?"

Sucking in a swift gulp of air, she nodded.

"Okay, um—first off, I'm gonna call for help. Then we're gonna get you out of here and into the back of my truck where I think you'll be more comfortable."

Again, all she could do was nod.

If Noah had thought his pulse was racing earlier, now he felt on the verge of passing out. He'd seen a lot of things in his years as county sheriff, but thankfully, he'd never happened upon a scene like this.

He reached his SUV in record time and radioed for an ambulance. The dispatcher patched him through to paramedics and after relaying what sketchy information he had, he dashed around to the back of his truck.

The rear door opened with a metallic screech, and Noah tossed aside the jack and jumper cables and spare jugs of wiper wash fluid, oil and water. He found the first-aid kit under the Bulldog bleacher pad he'd bought from one of his deputy's kids.

Next, he lowered the back seat into the flat position, then made a nest out of the stash of blankets he hadn't yet removed from that winter.

With the back seat down, he had a clear view of Kelsey's foil-wrapped wedding present on the front floorboard. Looked like something good had come from skipping out on the reception, since the contents of the box was a half-dozen ecru towels.

Ecru.

Now, who but Kelsey would ask for ecru towels?

Forcing Kelsey and the way she'd looked in her white satin gown from his mind, he dashed back to the Thunderbird.

"How're you doing?" he asked the woman inside, bum knee aching and slightly out of breath from adrenaline.

His heart sank when, once again, all he got from her was a weak nod.

"Okay, well, at least you're not worse. I'm going to open your door," he said, doing just that. "And then I'm going to lift you out of there." With the door open, he saw that she couldn't have been much over five feet. Good thing, since her car probably wouldn't hold anyone over five-three—and certainly not his own six-foot frame.

She wasn't wearing her seat belt, so he slipped his left hand beneath her knees and his right behind her back, easing her out of the car and deeper into his arms. She wore a black sundress, not all frilly and floral like the ones women wore in these parts, but severe in its shape.

All straight lines and business.

Even with the baby, she weighed nothing, and he cradled her close, mumbling something he hoped was comforting during the short walk to his truck.

In the fading sun, he noticed from the long silky waves kissing his left cheek that her hair wasn't mere red, but fire streaked with a hundred shades of blond. He'd never been big on hair colors beyond the basics, but even he could see that this gal's head was something special.

And her smell. Her perfume was a spicy, musky, sexy-hot Oriental blend that somehow matched the jade he remembered hiding behind her now closed eyes.

"You're gonna be just fine," he murmured, stopping just short of instinctively kissing her forehead. Geez, he'd been in law for twelve years and had yet to kiss one of the Jane Q. Publics he'd sworn to protect. Further proof that he shouldn't have come within three counties of Kelsey and Owen's big day.

His attraction meter was all screwed up.

At the back of his truck, Noah placed his good knee on the floorboard, then eased her inside, covering her with a blanket she pushed away.

"Hot—so hot," she said, voice scratchy and weak.

"Okay, um, let me see what I can do."

He'd just hopped down, planning to close up the

truck and turn on the A/C, when she reached for him, locking her fingers around his black leather belt.

"Please, stay," she said, eyes welling with tears just before she squeezed them shut and started funny panting breathing that felt way too intimate for him to witness. "I—I thought I could do this alone." She grimaced. "I do everything alone, but—" There she went with that breathing again. "Oh God, it hurts. Oh God, what am I going to do?" Somewhere in all of that, she'd raised her knees, then spread her legs wide, furrowing her lovely forehead with a grimace of what he could only guess was mind-numbing pain.

He matched that with his own case of vertigo.

Good Lord, she wasn't gonna have this baby right now, was she? He'd seen training videos on this sort of thing, but…

Suck it up, bud. This ain't no drill and you ain't no Boy Scout.

Noah looked over his shoulder for the ambulance, but no such luck.

"Okay, um, can you hold it?" he asked, taking yet another look.

"Nooooooo!" Thrashing her head from side to side, she emitted an otherworldly scream that startled a flock of crows into noisy flight.

Noah rolled up his sleeves and took a deep breath before assuming his usual professionalism. This was no longer about Kelsey, or his own fears, this was about saving this woman's life, and the life of her child.

"What's your name?" he said, knowing they were about to get real close—real fast.

"Cassandra—Cassie."

"Nice to meet you, Cassie. I'm Noah."

Though her beautiful face was all scrunched with pain, she nodded before cutting loose with another of her banshee wails. "It *huuuuurts!*" she cried.

"I know," he said, patting her knee. "I mean, obviously, I don't *know,* but—oh, man…"

I've gotta pull myself together.

Latex gloves. Definitely need those. Too bad the box of them was in the back of his county-issued Blazer.

Okay, so he had to somehow wash his hands. He was gonna need those towels, too.

Shooting into action, he grabbed the box with the towels, unwrapped it, then, stopping just short of pulling them out, he ran back around to the rear of the truck to grab one of the gallons of fresh water he kept on hand for busted radiators or the occasional dehydrated lost hiker.

In the first-aid kit, he fished out a couple of pre-packaged alcohol wipes, ripped one open with his teeth and scrubbed his hands as best as he could. Next, he poured water over them before giving his hands another good scrub.

Okay, now he was in business.

Hands clean, he grabbed a couple of the new-smelling towels and spread them under Cass's backside.

Another of her wails hurried him along.

She was now clutching at her dress, dragging it up lean, tan legs he had no business looking at, but had to. "My panties," she said. "T-they have to come off."

He nodded, then reached for the first-aid kit's scissors, and clinically snipped at robin's-egg-blue silk.

Oh boy—or girl!

There—right there between her legs was the crown of her baby's head!

"Okay, Cass, you're further into this than I thought." Grabbing her hand, he said, "Squeeze, darlin'. Squeeze me as hard as you can and push!"

Eyes wild, she did.

"Again," he said, keeping one eye on her and the other on the baby. Instinctively, he pushed her legs wider. "Push, Cassie, push. Come on, you can do it."

"Easy for you to say!" she snapped.

"That's right, darlin'—give me hell. Come on, I can take it! Give all men hell—especially your husband!"

"I—I'm—*arggghhh*—not married! I d-don't need a man!"

"Great, then I'll head back to town and grab a beer."

"No," she said through another grimace. "I do need you."

"Good," he said, eyes welling at the miracle unfolding before him. "Because a truckload of TNT couldn't tear me away from this spot. Push, darlin', push!"

"I'm trying!"

"Try harder!"

"I am—*arrrrgggghhhhh!*"

"Oh my God, I'm holding its head. Just a little more. A little *mooorre*. Got it. Oh my God," he said laughing through his tears. "It's a girl. You had a beautiful baby girl, Cassie!"

With his pinkie finger, he cleared the baby's mouth, and when the tiny, redheaded dream cut loose with a wail every bit as powerful as one of her momma's, with his spare hand he managed to spread a towel across Cassie's tummy before presenting her with her child—cord and all, which he planned on letting the paramedics cut.

Cassie's fiery hair hung in damp tendrils, and her complexion was misty with sweat, but never, in all of his days, had Noah seen a more beautiful, downright mesmerizing sight.

Then that gorgeous face of hers once again scrunched with pain.

"What's wrong?" he asked. "The baby's here."

"A-another one," she said with more pants. "Twins. Oh God, help me, please help me," she said, writhing her head from side to side, still clutching her baby girl. "*Noooo,* something's not right. It hurts—oh, it hurts!"

Heart hammering, Noah looked between her legs and not since seven years earlier on the night of that accident had he experienced such terror. Instead of a head, he saw a toe.

Sweet, merciful Heaven, why?

Okay, Noah…think.

Growing up in rural Arkansas, he had a lot of friends who'd lived on farms. He'd seen breech births with cattle—even a horse, but…

Okay, only difference is size. Sort of.

"It hurts, Noah! It hurts…" Cassie's agonized cries turned to racking sobs.

No. Not again.

Please Lord, don't let this be another night like that one on Blue Springs Road. I couldn't bear it. It wouldn't be right. That woman hadn't deserved to die, and You wouldn't let me save her. Just like Cassie, she'd had kids—a family.

Sure, Noah's friends had told him a hundred times over he hadn't been to blame, but by God, he'd been the one on the scene and he'd been the one holding her when she'd asked him to tell her husband and kids she loved them.

Too many times in his life, he'd been unable to fix things. It happened over and over in his job, then there'd been the messy breakup with Kelsey. Way before that, his folks' crappy marriage—or for that matter, his own. Not a damned one of those situations had he been able to fix. But this one…

With a light shake of his head, he told himself no. This wasn't going to be a replay of that night.

No one was taking this woman and her babies from him—not even almighty God Himself!

Fumbling across Cassie's still rounded belly, he felt the baby's head, and said, "I'm not gonna lie. This is probably—well, hell, there's no probably about it— this is gonna hurt real bad, and I'm sorry, but there's no other way."

Teeth gritted, she nodded, but her fire was gone, and her cries had faded to whimpers.

"Stay with me," he said, squeezing his eyes shut, frantically trying to remember that cheesy emergency labor video he and the guys laughingly winced their way through. Teeth gritted, he said a hundred more prayers in his head, then felt for one tiny foot, then the other, and gently tugged the baby by his or her ankles.

"Please don't let my baby die!"

"Nobody's dying here," he said. "Push!"

"I can't! I'm so tired."

"Push, dammit! Nobody's dying on my watch! I'm responsible for you—*all* of you. You hear me? Nobody's dyin' today! Now push!"

"I *caaaaaan't!*"

"That's it! I've got this little princess's behind. Come on, Cassie, give me all you got!"

Thankfully, she did, and he rotated the infant's trunk to get one arm. Another slight rotation earned him another.

"Come on, Cass! You're almost there!"

"*Arrrrggghhh!*" In one last superhuman effort, she pushed and the baby's head popped out.

Noah trembled so hard he feared dropping the second baby girl, but he held tight, reaching for another towel that he could hardly see through his tears.

He cleared the baby's mouth, and when she cried, he cried and started shaking all the harder. "You had another girl, darlin'. You did it."

Clutching both babies close, Cassie cast him a luminous smile before saying, "*We* did it. Thank you."

Bracing himself against the truck's frame, Noah shook his head and smiled.

Hot damn, what a rush.

Chapter Two

Cassie Tremont opened her eyes just enough to see hazy morning sun silhouetting one of the most handsome, kind and concerned faces she'd ever seen.

Noah.

Her savior. Her babies' savior.

Fast asleep in an orange vinyl guest chair he'd pulled to the head of her hospital bed. If only she'd come across a guy like him before meeting Tom, maybe her life would've turned out differently.

Maybe she'd even still believe in happy endings, because she wouldn't have had her dreams twice shattered by grim-faced company representatives standing at her front door. What were the odds of first, Tri-Comm reps telling her when she'd been just eight years old that her father had died of a heart attack while on the corporate jet. *Sorry. We're so sorry.* Then later, years later, Jubilee Cruise Lines reps telling her that not only had Tom, her husband, died, but he'd died on holiday with another woman. A woman who'd claimed to also be his wife! *We can only imagine your pain.*

Tom hadn't even been in the right country. He'd told

Cassie he was on a business trip to London. In reality, he'd been on a Caribbean cruise when he and his legal wife—a woman named Felicity—died in a freak diving accident.

The day Cassie had found out she was carrying twins, she'd been so happy—*they'd* been so happy. Tom had held her hand during the ultrasound, kissing the tips of her fingers, telling her she looked beautiful and was going to make the best mom in the world. His loving touch combined with the fierce love she already felt for the tiny miracles growing deep within her had made her teary with joy.

Even though the doctor warned Cassie that multiple births meant multiple risks, she hadn't cared. The only thing that mattered was that she and her beloved husband would soon have not one baby to love, but two.

She'd been twelve weeks pregnant when her world crashed around her. Tom's death had been hard enough to take, but hearing that their whole life together had been a lie—that was almost worse than knowing he was dead.

She'd been with Tom since college.

The night of her twenty-first birthday, when she'd taken legal possession of the millions her father left, Tom had proposed. She'd been so dewy-eyed with adoration for him, she'd taken his words of love at face value.

After all, why would he say he loved her if he didn't?

Little did she know, he'd been living a double life. With another wife.

Another house, car and cat.

How many times had she wished Tom were still alive? Not so she could hug him or kiss him or tell him how much she missed him, but so she could have the satisfaction of telling him how much she hated his guts!

Since the day she'd discovered the depth of Tom's deceptions, Cassie had immersed herself in the every-day running of her interior design firm. Her best friend and co-worker, Chloe, was constantly telling her to slow down, reminding her that she didn't have to work.

To which Cassie replied, no, she didn't *have* to work. She needed to. For if she slowed for even one second to think about all the laughs Tom and this Felicity woman must've had at her expense, she'd surely go stark raving mad!

For five idyllic years, she'd played house, while all that time Tom had been playing her for a fool!

Looking back on the past months, and especially the past week, from the perspective one gained after an uncomfortably close brush with death, Cassie guessed she should've paid closer attention when her doctor told her not to go on a business trip so close to her due date.

But since Tom's death, Cassie prided herself on controlling everything.

Guess in this case, Mother Nature got the last laugh.

Eyeing Noah again, she yawned. Not because anything about him was remotely boring, but because something about just having him here with her in the room filled her with an uncharacteristic feeling of peace. One she hadn't felt since the last time she'd fallen asleep in his arms.

NOAH LOOKED UP when the door to Cassie's room burst open and a nurse wheeled in a baby on a cart.

"How's our mommy doing?" the heavyset woman asked.

"Still pretty out of it."

"That's to be expected," she said, making a clucking sound that matched the baby ducks splashed all over her yellow surgical scrubs. "She had a rough delivery, but she'll be fine now." Leaving the clear plastic bassinet with the baby near the sink, the nurse washed her hands before bustling over to the bed. "Ms. Tremont, I know you're still tired, but your babies need breakfast. We've been in touch with your OB/GYN in Little Rock and she said you're planning on breastfeeding?"

Eyes closed, the weary patient nodded.

"Okay, then, I'm sorry to do this, but you have to wake up." The nurse lightly shook Cassie's shoulder.

"B-but…" Cass licked her dry lips, and Noah reached for the tube of Chapstick he'd bought her in the hospital gift shop, gliding some on. With the tip of her tongue, she traced his balmy line.

Noah swallowed hard.

How come Cassie merely licking her lips had resulted in immediate below-the-belt action?

Sleep. Had to be lack of sleep.

Only possible explanation.

"It's okay, darlin'," he finally found the air to say,

holding her left hand while speaking into her thick hair. "Time to rise and shine."

"Do I have to?"

The nurse laughed. "You can't imagine how many of my new mommies say the same thing. Come on now, Ms. Tremont, time to wake up. Your adorable babies need their first meal."

"Maybe Cass needs something to eat?" Noah suggested.

"She'll be fine," the nurse said with a sharp, authoritarian tone.

Well, excuse me for asking. Checking that his tiny princess hadn't been frightened by the nurse's bark, Noah eyed his baby girl. Lucky for Nurse Nasty she contentedly continued her nap.

"Most of our new mommies are a little out of it, but Ms. Tremont, here, had an extra tough time."

"Tell me about it," he said under his breath.

"You the father?"

"No, I—"

"Well, then, you'll have to leave. Patient privacy and all."

"I don't think so." *With me gone, who's gonna keep an eye on you, Nurse Nasty?*

"Please, sir. Ms. Tremont really does need to get on with the business of mothering. While nursing is a natural, beautiful part of that process, the patient will undoubtedly want her privacy." The nurse handed a pink bundle to Cass.

Nursing? Noah scratched his head. What was this

woman talking about? Cassie couldn't even get out of bed. How was she going to—oh.

That kind of nursing.

The kind with babies and *breasts*.

I'm outta here!

Noah leaned over the bed rail to kiss Cassie's forehead, then the baby's. "I'll uh, be around," he said, giving Cassie's hand a final squeeze. "Just holler if you need me. Not that you will. I mean, I'm sure you can handle this on your own. But you know how—"

"I know," she said, wide eyes glowing from the intensity of her adorable sleepy grin. "Go on. Get. I'll be fine."

Sure, she'd be fine, but what about him?

Those spur-of-the-moment kisses had been a mistake!

Cassie's grin had him all hot and cold and maybe even dizzy. And all of that was before he'd made the mistake of kissing her baby! The kid smelled confusing. Like sweetness and innocence and baby lotion and shampoo. But then underlying that was Cass's exotic oriental perfume—that spicy, musky, sexy, sultry storm of mixed signals designed for no good reason other than landing him in serious bachelor trouble.

Okay, deep breaths.

There's nothing to be alarmed about.

He hadn't slept in what? Like eighteen hours? Surely lack of sleep was bound to mess with a guy's head?

"Noah?" Cassie asked, voice ripe with concern.

"Are you okay? All of a sudden you don't look so good."

"Sure…I'm, ah, great." He swallowed hard, ran his fingers around the already loose collar of the dress shirt he had yet to change out of. "Probably just need some shut-eye."

"Of course, you do. Poor thing, you've been here all night. I'm fine. Why don't you go home and get some sleep?"

Great idea!

While Cassie was still recovering, honor would never permit him to leave her of his own free will. But since Nurse Nasty was still giving him the evil eye, and Cassie had told him to leave, and not to mention the fact that she was about to bare her breasts, Noah made a final round of kisses, then high-tailed it out of the room.

"THAT'S QUITE A MAN you've got there," the nurse said to Cassie while making a note on her chart.

"Thanks, but Noah's not my man. He's my guardian angel."

And speaking of angels…

The sleeping angel Cassie held in her arms took her breath away. Had there ever been a more beautiful sight?

Apple-blossom-pink cheeks and a tiny scrunched nose. And that shock of red curls! Guess those old wives' tales about heartburn had been right!

Emotion swelling, Cassie blinked back tears.

For the miracle she now held in her arms, every bit

of the anguish she'd been through over Tom had been worth it.

Not only was she alive, but she was holding her very much alive baby in her arms, with another perfect baby waiting in line for her breakfast, as well.

And just think, she had this double blessing and her own life all because of Noah. Though the actual delivery of her babies had become a blur, he was the one thing about her ordeal that she'd never forget. His soothing voice, and the way he'd held her hand, urging her not to give up.

Starting at the still-warm spot on her forehead where Noah had planted his tender kiss, a quiet contentment crept through her.

"Given any thought to names?" the nurse asked, reading the card on a pink carnation bouquet.

Of course. Since Tom's death, Cassie planned her days down to the minute, and since the end of her second trimester she'd known the girls would be named Rachel, after her mother, and Ruth, after her grandmother, but now...

Now she wasn't so sure.

"Was this baby born first?" Cassie asked, gazing at the infant in her arms.

The nurse nodded, reading the cards on lilac and then peach roses.

"Then she'll be Noelle."

The nosy nurse smiled and nodded approvingly. "And her sister?"

"I don't know." Cassie grinned, skimming her finger along Noelle's tiny strawberry-blond brows. "I think I'll just dream up something when I meet her."

Noelle woke with a start, scrunching her mouth into a full-blown squall.

"I take it that means she's hungry?"

The nurse nodded before talking Cassie through the breastfeeding procedure.

Far from what the many books Cassie had read on nursing had told her, there was nothing simple about it! Still, after a few rough starts, by the time the nurse brought in Cassie's second baby, then left mother and daughter on their own, Cassie felt like an old pro.

Now that her latest diner had eaten her fill, then promptly fallen back to sleep, Cassie took her time memorizing her dear face—not hard since she looked exactly like her sister!

"What should I name you?" she asked, smoothing her hand over her second daughter's silken crown.

A knock sounded on the door, and Cassie looked up. "Come in."

"Hey. How's it going? Everyone decent?" Noah popped his head around the edge of the oversized door.

"Hi," Cassie said, unprepared for the rush of warmth flooding her system on hearing his voice—let alone meeting his warm, brown gaze and easy smile.

"Hi." The paper rustling of shopping bags bursting with gifts preceded him into the room.

"What in the world?"

He dumped his purchases on the room's spare bed. "Thought you and the girls might need a few things." Out came matching Malibu Barbies and tea sets and stuffed bunnies and ducks and rattles and teething key rings and pink, purple and yellow dresses with ruffled skirts bigger than both babies combined.

"A *few* things?" Cassie laughed. "Noah, from the looks of it you've got the girls set up with enough gear to last them from infancy straight through to college."

Drawing the guest chair away from the window to the head of her bed, he shrugged. "I figure what can it hurt to plan ahead?"

While he sat, she grinned. "Tea sets, Noah? They can't even sit up."

"What can I say? They were on sale."

His easy smile stole any further protests she might have launched. And then his expression turned strangely serious. Leaning forward, he reached for her closest hand, enfolding it in his.

She swallowed hard, willing her pulse to slow.

"I'm so glad you and the girls are out of the woods," he said. "I know all of these presents must seem like overkill, but I'm just so damned relieved."

"Me, too," Cassie said, licking her lips. "I'm not sure how I'll ever repay you."

"Your smile is all the thanks I need."

"Yes, well…" Suddenly shy, and unsure of the complex emotions that made the back of her throat ache, Cassie gave his hand a quick squeeze before releasing him. "That might be good enough for you," she finally managed to say. "But I'm going to think of something more grand."

He cleared his throat. "Like naming Noelle for me

wasn't already a pretty grand gesture? They put her name on a card in front of her bassinet.''

"Who said she was named for you?'' Cassie teased with a sassy wink.

"Ouch." Noah clutched his chest. "Talk about zinging an arrow straight through my heart.''

After they'd shared another laugh, he reverently feathered his fingers across her baby's curls, reminding Cassie of how good that same touch had felt to her yesterday afternoon in the back of his SUV.

Squeezing her eyes briefly shut, she returned to that moment. To the wonder of being cocooned in Noah's strength. Even though today his comforting hand touched her baby, his kindness still managed to touch her soul.

"So?" he asked. "You come up with a name for this one yet?''

"Nope."

"Hmm…how about Joelle?''

Nose wrinkled, Cassie said, "Thanks, but I don't think so.''

"No rhymes?''

She shrugged. "Rhymes are okay, but I thought keeping the N-theme might be nice.''

"Okay…*N, N*—Nicky, Nancy, Nathan—''

"Oh, now, Nathan. That'd be real cute embroidered on her ballerina costumes.''

He made a face. "Hey, at least I'm trying. I don't hear any brilliant ideas coming from you.''

"True." Drawing in her lower lip, she said, "Nobody told me having babies turns your mind to mush.''

''Give me that kid,'' he said, reaching for the baby girl, then holding her close. She looked so tiny in his arms. So safe.

Noah was a big man.

Like Cassie's father had been.

Growing up, Cassie had worshipped him. When her mother died of cancer before Cass had been barely old enough to talk, her father had meant the world to her. He'd been someone big and strong to protect her from the rough and tumble world. In Tom, she thought she'd found someone much like her own powerful dad. Even in school, her then future husband had possessed a magnetic presence. Just looking at him, she'd known he was destined for greatness. Sure enough, right out of law school, he'd landed a job with a top Little Rock firm. Everyone loved him—his partners, his clients, and his two wives.

One ''wife'' might still be alive—but Cassie's love wasn't. It had long since turned to hate, and even thinking Tom's name turned her blood cold.

Having been raised by her overprotective Aunt Olivia, Cassie had always thought if only she'd had her mom and dad with her for a little while longer, her life would have turned out differently. Maybe then she wouldn't have run straight into Tom's scheming arms.

Trouble was, she had. And looking back on it, for all the wrong reasons. Fear over not being able to make her own way in the world. Reluctance to be alone. Being so eager to start her own family, that she'd never even considered the fact that the man she thought she loved had been a con artist extraordinaire.

All of those reasons combined had since taught her a valuable life lesson. That fairy tales were better left to the experts at Disney. For in real life, when it came to relationships with men, there was no such thing as happily ever after.

Now, relationships with babies on the other hand…

"She sure smells good," Noah said, nuzzling the baby's downy soft hair. "How 'bout giving her a flower name? Petunia or Hydrangea?"

Cassie made a face. "Still not quite right."

He shifted the infant from where she'd rested her tiny head against his chest to cradle her in his arms. Putting the tip of his long index finger to her nose, he said, "You gave me one heck of a scare, young lady."

"Me, too," Cassie said, queasy at just the memory of how dicey her second child's birth had been.

"Now, I look at you," Noah said to the tiny infant, "and all I see is hope. Hope for a very bright future filled with giggles and sunshine and water balloon fights and puppies and—"

"Hope," Cassie said. "That's it."

"What?"

"Her name. I'll call her Hope."

"Wait a minute, don't I get a say in this? After all, I was the one who ushered her into this world."

"True. So, if you don't like that, then what do you suggest?"

"There's always Joelle."

"Noah!"

"Don't get your diaper in a wad," he said, his wide

smile aimed straight for her heart. "I was just razzing you. Hope sounds perfect."

Perfect... Cassie thought with a secret smile.

Just like my new friend, Noah, who not only gave both of my daughters their lives, but names.

"PSST. ARE YOU AWAKE?"

Cassie cracked open one eye to see a model-perfect, blue-eyed brunette staring at her—a very pregnant perfect brunette. When Cassie opened both eyes, the woman held out her hand for her to shake.

"Oh, good," she said. "You are awake. I'm Tiffany. Number Three in Noah's Lonely Hearts Support Group, formed way back in the early nineties. When Noah's ex-wife, Darla, decided marriage bored her, Noah decided he felt the same. Since then, we've grown considerably. The woman we all thought he'd marry, Kelsey, is Number Seventeen. He's dated casually after her—no one significant enough for a number, but you, my dear, show promise, and as such, we've already assigned you Number Eighteen. Since I'm on maternity leave from Olivetti's—that's Riverdale's best dress shop if you happen to need anything while you're in town—I've been nominated by the group to welcome you."

Cassie's look must have been blank, because unfortunately the woman continued while her crisp, outdoorsy perfume filled the room.

"No need to look shocked," she said, "like your babies have been bugged or anything. We have inside sources all over town. At the hospital, Noah dated

Nurse Helen—she's Number Eleven amongst his victims.''

"His victims?''

"Yeah, you know, his Victims in Love—or VILs as we affectionately call 'em. Here,'' Tiffany said, reaching into a quilted blue toile purse to pull out a gold foil box. "The girls and I bought you a combination Congratulations on Your Babies/Welcome to the Group gift. I know this must seem a bit premature, offering you membership when you and Noah have only just met, but after what happened at Kelsey's wedding, we figure Noah's gotta be on the verge of a total meltdown. Now, the women around here are equipped to handle his many bad boy charms, but we figure you being a city girl, may need a few pointers to come out of this on the right side of sanity.''

"Um, thank you,'' Cassie said, taking the box of Godiva chocolates. "I think.''

"Oh dear,'' Tiffany said with a pretty frown.

"What?'' The severity of her tone tempted Cassie to check herself for broken bones.

"Your expression—sour as a lemon drop. You're not already hooked on Noah, are you?''

"I don't think so. I barely know the man.''

Sagely nodding, Tiffany said, "That's what we all said. Every last one of us believed we'd be the ones to finally hog-tie him, but he's wily when it comes to commitment. Darla hurt him bad, and I'm warning you, you so much as breathe the word and he'll bolt. It's our belief that Kelsey had him so long because we'd precounseled her on this fact. Since she already had that heads-up, she knew better than to ever even ask about taking their relationship to that magical, mystical place we group members call marriage. But then she just had to go and give him that ultimatum, and bam—faster than that tornado we had back in 1998, he was gone."

Interesting…

The supposedly heartbroken woman's perfectly manicured red nails were attached to long, tanned fingers sporting an array of not-too-shabby rings. One in particular on her left hand was at least a two-carat square-cut diamond solitaire with matching bejeweled wedding band.

Mind you, Cassie was no expert, but those looked like some serious love baubles to her! This in mind, she blurted, "But you're married now, aren't you?"

"Mm-hmm…" A look of utter bliss drifted over Tiffany's classically beautiful features as she patted her bulging tummy through her cornflower-blue linen dress. "Noah's 'It's not you, it's me' speech really did a number on my self-esteem. I thought we'd been in love, when all along it turns out I was the only participant in the love part of our relationship—if you could even call it that. Anyway, Denton Harwood, school math club president and heir to the First National Bank of Riverdale, took pity on me and we've been together ever since."

"Congratulations," Cassie said, fighting back a smile. Was this woman and all seventeen of her friends nuts?

"Thank you. I've never been happier, which is why I'm giving you a friendly warning to be careful."

"Oh, I will," Cassie said, more to get this nutcase out of her room than because of any fears she had of Noah breaking her heart.

In the first place, after what Tom had done to her, she no longer had a heart when it came to men. And in the second, no matter how handsome he was, or kind and considerate, Noah was only her friend. Period.

"Good," Tiffany said, patting Cassie's leg through two layers of cotton blankets. "Deep down, Noah's a great guy, but he has definite commitment issues. With you just having had twins and all, we would hate to see you caught off guard when you become his eighteenth VIL."

When Tiffany and her perfume had safely left the room, Cassie rolled her eyes.

The woman might think she knew Noah, but obviously she didn't. Because if there was one thing Cassie had learned during her brief stay in Riverdale, it was the fact that Sheriff Noah Wheeler was as committed as men come!

"DON'T YOU EVER go to work?"

Late that afternoon, Noah glanced up from the bass fishing magazine he'd been reading in Cassie's guest chair—the one he'd once again had to move from its usual spot by the window to the head of her bed where he could keep a closer eye on her. "You're awake."

"And you're still here." Her sleepy grin took the sting out of her words.

"That a problem?" he asked, chest tight with pride—not to mention relief—over the fact that his patient looked healthier by the hour.

"No…" She looked down, pinch-pleating the white sheet. "It's just that we hardly know each other, yet you've moved in. I've gotten used to being on my own."

"That my cue to beat it?" Damn if that sleep-sexy grin of hers wasn't already revving his engine.

She laughed. "Not at all. You've been a godsend in so many ways, but the nurse said we'll probably be going home tomorrow, so I figure you'll be glad to get back to your normal schedule."

"I suppose. But it's not like police work in these parts is all that exciting. I get more of a rush out of helping someone with a flat tire than writing tickets."

"Sure. You would."

"What's that mean?"

"That you're a nice guy."

Noah frowned.

When it came to women, nice guys *always* finished last. His busted relationship with Kelsey proved it!

Still, since he wasn't even remotely attracted to Cass, he supposed in her case friendship was a good thing. A safe thing. "So," he said, "when do you think they'll spring you? I'll need to pick up car seats and fasten them into my truck."

"Why?"

Leaning forward, he said, "Well, it's a sure bet the four of us aren't going to fit in your car—not to mention the fact that no matter how healthy you look, it's a long trip to Little Rock. You're still on the mend. No way you should be driving.''

''Um—'' she drew in her lower lip ''—not that I don't appreciate your offer, but early this morning I contacted a limo service in Fayetteville. They'll arrive tomorrow at noon. They'll also handle the transport of my car.''

''Oh.'' Like a deflated balloon, he sagged against the chair. So, she'd hired a limo? Big deal. What did he care? This was a good thing, right?

Ha!

Then how come he felt like he'd just gotten dumped?

Gaze all wide-eyed and innocent, she said, ''You look upset.''

He shook his head.

''Noah? Please tell me what's wrong.'' Her gentle tone ripped right through him.

''You wanna know what's wrong, Cass? I'll tell you. It's customary for the father to drive his kids home— not some hired limo service.''

''But you're not Noelle and Hope's father.''

He hardened his jaw.

''You seem surprised, as if this is news to you.''

''Look,'' he said, resting his elbows on his knees. ''You and those girls very nearly died out on that high-way. Once I happened upon you, and saw what kind of trouble you were in, you—all of you—became my responsibility. A responsibility I don't take lightly.''

She reached for his hand, and gave him a surprisingly strong squeeze. ''Never will you know the depth of my gratitude. Never will I be able to repay you for helping me like you did. And I suppose that kind of intensity breeds a strange kind of instant intimacy, but the crisis is over, Noah. I'm fine. The girls are fine. And tomorrow we're going home.''

''I'm glad. Truly I am. I just wanted to make sure you got home safely. You know, complete the circle where you're concerned.''

When she released his hand to tuck luxurious red waves behind her ears, unexpected—unwanted—loneliness invaded his gut. Kelsey had left him, and that'd felt bad. Now, Cassie was leaving, too? That felt even worse. No. He didn't want her letting go of his hand any more than he wanted her and her babies going home.

Good Lord, someone call 9-1-1!

A bachelor afraid of spending a little quality time on his own was not a good thing.

''I appreciate your concern,'' she said, sending him deeper into emotional and now physical turmoil by licking her full lips. *Down, boy, down.* ''Especially since it's not likely we'll ever see each other again.''

''Sure.''

Wait a minute... She was right!

What could his bachelorhood status possibly have to fear from Cassie since after today he'd never see her again? Finally. A voice of reason—welcome, even if it wasn't in his own head!

Yeah, but tell me, Einstein—what's her leaving going to do for your loneliness?

Noah swallowed hard.

That inner voice was nothing more than lingering shame over Kelsey having dumped him. Oh—not to mention sleep deprivation. Obviously, he must still be a little weak. Easily enough remedied next weekend when he'd have a whole Saturday of shut-eye followed by a Sunday all-male barbecue. Yep, get all the guys out on his just-finished backyard deck, all gathered around his brand spanking new gas grill for some ribs, burgers and beers.

Yep, hot damn, life just didn't get any better than that. Just as soon as he got Cassie and company home, he'd start making calls.

So as not to appear too eager to get her out of town, he said, "I remember you saying you're not married, so when you get home, who's going to watch out for you? Mom, dad? Friends? Ex?"

Had he only imagined the catch in her breath as she shook her head? "I'm the only family my girls will ever need. I'll be a mother to tuck them in at night. A father to play baseball, and a favorite aunt to take them to the zoo. And when they're teenagers, needing a close friend to confide in, I'll be that, too."

"Sounds like you've got your lives mapped out."

"I do. And if you were an explorer and happened upon us, and wanted to give our happy little family a name, wanna guess what it would be?"

"Wouldn't have a clue."

"No Man's Land."

Had Noah been fully awake, Cass's declaration would have sounded like heaven to his female-wary ears. But in his obviously still sleep-weakened condition, her blunt speech sounded defensive.

Someone had hurt her. Bad. Question was, what—if anything—was he going to do about it?

Chapter Three

After Noah left, if Cassie hadn't already been in bed, she'd have collapsed. What had gotten into her to say such an outrageous thing?

Maybe the quiet thrill of his gentle kiss? The security of having his hand around yours? Seeing your tiny baby sheltered in his big, strong arms, and wondering how much richer your daughters' lives would be than your own if, unlike you, they grew up with a father?

Cassie frowned.

That was ridiculous!

The last thing her girls needed was a daddy. Besides, Cassie was no more interested in Noah than he was in her.

So why did she get all defensive on him?

Tom. That's why.

Because his lies had forever and irrevocably changed her for the worse. More than ever she hated her former husband for instilling in her an innate need for constructing emotional walls.

Where her heart had once contained nothing but

trusting naiveté, now, she knew she'd never trust another man again—not of choice, but necessity.

On her own, she'd barely survived Tom's deception, but now, she had the girls' well-being to consider.

Noah seemed like a nice guy. Yet Tiffany claimed he ran when the word *commitment* was so much as breathed around him. So why was he still hanging around?

Baffling. The man's actions were utterly baffling.

Putting her hands to her temples, Cassie tried massaging answers from her aching head.

Why was this virtual stranger being so darned nice?

What did he want from her?

Even more disturbing, what did she want from him?

She would have pondered all of the questions further, but ever since delivering the babies, her mind and body had had a tough time coordinating schedules.

This time, her body won, and sleep stealthily took hold.

"THAT'S OKAY, Doctor," Cassie said early the next morning after he'd lightly shaken her awake from her latest nap. "I understand about the girls needing to stay on." What she didn't understand was why no one in this hospital wanted her to sleep!

"All right, then…" said the pediatrician caring for the twins. His black toupee hung a bit askew from the gray tufts peeking around the sides, but his friendly smile lit the blue eyes behind his gold-rimmed glasses. "If our craft fair makes it tough for you to find a room, let me know, and I'll see what I can do."

"Thanks," Cassie said, "but I'm sure I'll manage just fine."

Hugging the babies' charts, Doctor Joe, as he liked to be called, paused on his way out the door to give her a thumbs-up. "Young lady, judging by the spunk it must've taken to bring those two girls into this world, I'm sure you will."

Famous last words.

Ever since the doctor had informed Cassie that she was free to leave the hospital, but her babies weren't, due to a mild case of jaundice, she'd been dialing her way through Riverdale's meager yellow pages, trying to find a hotel, motel or even a houseboat for rent.

Unfortunately, every single establishment she'd called had had only one thing to say. "Sorry, but because of the craft fair, we've been booked for months."

Even down in Little Rock, she'd heard of the twice annual northwest Arkansas event. She even had friends who regularly made the trip for handwoven baskets, hand-strung beaded necklaces and funnel cakes. What Cassie hadn't known was just what a big deal the craft extravaganza actually was.

Oh sure, this early in the week, she could've gotten a room in Fayetteville, Springdale or Rogers, but for only two nights. What if the babies ended up staying longer? And how was she going to manage the hundred and twenty mile round trip commute?

Just as she'd hung up on Doxy's Motor court after yet another apology, a knock sounded on her door.

"Come in," she sang out, glad she'd at least managed to put on *real* clothes in between calls.

At least two dozen yellow roses arranged in an elegant crystal vase walked in attached to long, strong masculine legs encased in faded jeans. "Good morning," said a familiar voice that sounded an awful lot like Noah from behind the fragrant blooms. "I brought you a going-away gift."

"If only I had somewhere to go," she said, trying not to pout. "I don't suppose you have any connections with the local inns?"

"What's this? Miss Independence is actually asking for help?" Noah set the flowers and his keys on the bedside table, then lowered himself into his usual chair. The red Razorback T-shirt he'd changed into did the most amazing tricks with his warm brown eyes, and his dark hair looked all spiky and damp from a recent shower.

Cheeks warming at the mere thought of him all rock hard and suds slick, she hastily looked away.

Trying to ignore the heady scent of the roses, not to mention the completely irrational quickening of her pulse, Cassie stuck out her tongue before saying, "Thank you for the flowers. They're beautiful."

"You're welcome. And might I say you look particularly fetching yourself—all dressed up in your fancy black dress, but with nowhere to go, huh?"

"Thanks again for reminding me." From her perch on the edge of the bed, she wrinkled her nose. "Guess the nurses told you I get to go home, but Noelle and Hope are staying."

He nodded. "Nurse Helen said this jaundice thing is fairly common."

"Oh, she did, did she?" What had been Helen's support group initiation number? Eleven? "You two getting cozy?"

"Jealous?"

Yes!

No! Of course not!

Seeing how Cassie didn't even want a man in her life, let alone need one, she wished the buxom nurse all the luck in the world in resnagging the handsome sheriff. After all, Tiffany hadn't said anything about group members not being able to launch new Noah campaigns.

"I'm not a bit jealous," she finally said, tucking her long hair firmly behind her ears. "Merely making conversation. Your friend Tiffany stopped by yesterday, and told me all about the support group they formed to get over you—you big stud."

When she winked, Noah looked sharply away.

"Don't worry," she said. "Even though I barely know you, I can see the man she told me about and you have nothing in common. Those women obviously have too much time on their hands. Anyway, back to my lodging issue—know anyplace that might have a room?" She flashed him a hopeful grin.

"Um, sure." Though he was mighty pleased to no longer be hearing about that ridiculous support group, Noah cringed inwardly when another of his hot-cold dizzy spells accompanied her latest innocent question. Damn those gorgeous eyes of hers. And she could knock off the grinning, too. Unfortunately, yes, he did know of a place to stay. Trouble was, inviting her to use it violated every rule he'd spent years perfecting.

"Well? The name?"

"You probably wouldn't want to stay there. It's, um, pretty messy."

"So? I'll clean it."

"No, I mean *really* messy. Downright unsanitary. You might, ah, catch something."

Fixing him with a laser beam stare, she narrowed her gaze. "Why do I get the feeling wherever this place is, you don't want me there?"

"That's crazy." He gulped.

How had Cassie known exactly what he was thinking? Did she also know how rotten he felt about those thoughts? After all, he'd promised to protect her until she was released from the hospital. And since she *was* being released, then technically, he was released from all obligation, right? So why did he still feel like a schmuck for not wanting her in his home?

Probably because you do *want her? All of her lush little curves and big, green Saturday-morning-sex eyes and that damned adorable grin that keeps turning you all hot and dizzy.*

Solely to prove that none of that was even remotely true—well, granted some of it was, but certainly not the part about him wanting her—Noah blurted, "Look, I've got a guest room. You want it, or not?"

"Yes, please. If it's not too much trouble." She grinned, and in the heart of his bachelor's gut, he died ten thousand hot and dizzy deaths.

"Nope. No trouble at all." What was wrong with him? He'd gone without sleep before, but never had it affected him like this.

Could he have contracted some swift-acting deadly disease? Yeah. That was it. Had to be. No other way would he be this upset over a little bitty snippet of a woman with a pretty smile and even prettier face wreathed in the most prettiest red hair.

Argh! *Most prettiest?* Whatever sickness he had, looked like it was growing more serious by the second!

"Oh, Noah, thank you!" She leaned entirely too close, grazing her full breasts against his chest while wrapping her arms around his neck in a hug. And as if that wasn't bad enough, she finished him off with an all-too-innocent kiss to his cheek. His cheek! After the anguish her eyes and that grin of hers had put him through, at the very least he deserved a taste of those ripe lips—not to mention a taste of that naughty darting tongue! Her flaming, kiss-shaped brand still burning his left cheek, she said, "You're the best friend a girl could ever have."

Friend?

Damn. But then wait—where he and Cassie were concerned, friendship was a good thing. It proved he had a virus rather than the hots for her.

"Um, thanks," he said, "Coming from you, Cass, I'll take that as a compliment. Do you mind if I call you Cass?"

She beamed and shook her head. He grew warm.

Dizzy.

I have to get out of here. Now!

Because he wasn't feeling sick, but attracted. And proud and fiercely protective. And he'd had lots of friends in his life, but none of them he'd wanted to draw back into his arms and kiss square on her soft, full lips!

"Noah? You all right? You're looking pale again."

"Sure," he said, swallowing hard. "I'm fine. Great. Never been better."

"Good. So? Ready to head over to your place?"

"You know, I just remembered a couple errands I have to run. Let me do those, and I'll be back."

"Why don't I go with you? I'm not due back for a feeding until this afternoon, and after being laid up in here I could sure use a change in scenery."

Sure. That was all he needed, to be cooped up in the car with her and that Oriental perfume he'd long since established to be trouble. "You know," he finally said. "I would love to take you, but, um, official sheriff's code of Pritchett County states that I can't have any noncriminal civilian passengers in my county-owned vehicle."

"Oh."

"You just hang tight. I'll be back to get you in my SUV around two."

"Okay. Sure. That'd be great."

Without so much as a wave, he was gone, leaving Cassie wondering if she'd said something to upset him. But then not five minutes later he was back—wearing an even fiercer frown than the one he'd left with.

"Need these?" she asked, jangling his keys. She held them out, but just when he reached for them, she snatched them back. "Not so fast, mister. You were in an awfully big hurry to get out of here."

"Yeah, so?"

"So... You're not still upset over that support group, are you?"

A muscle ticked in his jaw.

"I'll take that as a yes."

"Actually, I was about to say no. But since we're on the subject, let's get one thing straight." He'd taken his voice dangerously low. "Those women might say they were the ones who got hurt, but they'd be lying. I did darned good by every one of them. I'd thought we had something special, but then they had to—"

Bring up the word *commitment?* "What, Noah? What did they do?"

He raked his fingers through his hair, sighed, then grabbed his keys while she was staring into his eyes instead of at his hands. "I'll be back around two."

FIFTEEN MINUTES LATER, Noah claimed a counter stool at Brenda's Bigger Burger.

Brenda herself, order pad in her plump hand and wearing one of the dozens of psychedelic muumuus she'd picked up on last summer's trip with her sister to Maui, ambled out from the kitchen. "What can I get for you, Sheriff?"

"Got any new lives stashed back there?"

"Aw, surely things can't be that bad. After all, talk is you're a new daddy. Babies always bring a good-some dose of joy."

"Unless they're snake babies." Ernie, Brenda's

cook and husband, peeked through the kitchen's pass-thru. "Homer Claussen found a whole nest of copperheads out in his south pasture."

"You don't say…" Noah nodded. Experience had long since taught him it was far better to go along with whatever Ernie said. Any contradictions, and the four-foot, ten-inch former pro wrestler tended toward belligerence.

"Yep. Hundreds of 'em wrapped all around his best calf. Nearly squooze him half to death. Homer called the vet, but she said there wasn't a thing she could do."

"You're so making that up," Brenda said.

"Am not! Call over to Homer's and see. His wife'll tell you every word is true."

See? Noah closed his eyes, wishing Brenda would've just gone along with Ernie's latest outrageous tale. Now, he'd have to listen to this bickering all the way through his lunch. And Lord, how he hated bickering. Brenda and Ernie were just one more shining example of why m-marriage doesn't work. He had no trouble seeing it. So why did all the other men and women of the world still seem confused?

"Can I get you your usual Coke, double cheeseburger and Tater Tots?" Brenda asked during fight intermission—meaning Ernie must've taken a time-out to grab a fresh bag of something from the freezer.

"Why don't you change that Coke to a chocolate malt?"

Brenda frowned. "Tiffany stopped by here awhile ago and said those women of yours already gave your babies' momma an official group number. She's Ms. Eighteen. Things that serious already, huh?''

Noah washed his face with his hands.

This whole town was a few donuts short of a dozen!

Wonder if the Fayetteville police force was doing any hiring?

In a back booth, a trio of teenaged girls burst into giggles.

He hadn't thought the idea of moving to Fayetteville all that funny.

Just as he didn't cotton to their skipping classes. He was just rising off of his stool to go over and say something when he realized they were out on their lunch break, and sat back down.

''Yo, Sheriff!''

Noah didn't even have to glance toward the burger joint's opening door to know his youngest deputy, Jimmy Groves, was heading his way.

''Briggs has been looking for ya.''

''Oh, yeah?'' Noah said above the racket Brenda was making with the malt machine. ''What's he want?'' Briggs was another deputy—the complete opposite of tall, lean and young Jimmy. Briggs didn't have any hair, was a single parent to three great girls and one boy, and spent his every waking moment when he wasn't on patrol or ferrying said kids watching tapes of Martha Stewart. Briggs had loved his wife to a dangerous degree. When she'd died of complications of diabetes, folks round town said Briggs would die right along with her. Still one more reason Noah wanted no part of marriage.

Far from being a blessing, loving a woman to that degree sounded more like a curse. Thank goodness Briggs and his munchkin crew seemed to be doing okay, two years later.

"He thought it might be nice to wash your girl-friend's car. You know, that hot yellow Thunderbird?"

Noah rolled his eyes while Brenda set his malt on the gold-speckled counter in front of him.

He took a long, slow drink, savoring the icy goodness that eased fiery indigestion no doubt brought on by all this talk about him and Cass having already formed some kind of bond. Couldn't everyone see they were nothing more than friends?

"First off," he said, "Cassie's hardly my girl—just the mother of my babies, which technically aren't even mine, but—oh hell, you know what I mean. And second, stay away from her car."

"But it's awfully dusty."

"Jimmy…"

"Come on, Sheriff, *pleeeease*. Briggs got to drive it all the way into town from out on the highway, and all I got to do was sit behind the wheel once she was already parked." Jimmy was one of those kids who had posters of cars up on his bedroom walls instead of bikini-clad women. "If you'll let me just drive it real slow to the car wash, I promise I'll never ask for anything else."

"No."

Dragging his lip like a kid who'd got nothing for Christmas, Jimmy slinked out of Brenda's and back to the sheriff's office located five doors down across the street.

Why was it that the more Noah thought about Cassie and the hornet's nest of women supposedly scorned, the more he wished she'd had those babies of hers in someone else's town?

"THIS IS NICE," Cassie said after Noah had given her the grand tour of his cozy four-bedroom ranch home. She'd decided not to mention the fact that after having told her back at the hospital that he wasn't allowed to have civilian passengers in his county-issued Blazer, he'd turned around and picked her up in it!

"Thanks. I can't really take any of the credit, though. Mom did all of the homey stuff. Dad and I just did our part to help keep everything clean."

"So what happened?" Cassie asked with a smile twinkling in her eyes. While the house wasn't trashed, in spite of pretty blue floral curtains, mossy green walls and an antique china cabinet brimming with dusty, rose-patterned china, the place definitely had the look and feel of a bachelor pad.

Dirty dishes filled the sink, and mail, newspapers and grocery store sales circulars cluttered the white tile kitchen counters. A dirty frying pan had been left on the stove. Bread crumbs dusted the counter beside it, along with a butter knife and one of those plastic wraps off of a slice of American cheese.

On the living room floor resided hiking boots, an array of video games scattered in front of the jumbo TV and plenty of dirty towels, T-shirts and socks. The overstuffed brown leather sofa was missing a cushion—never mind. There it was, beside the PlayStation II. An earth-toned plaid recliner held a basket of clothes. Judging by the fabric softener sheets crowning the pile, Cassie figured they were clean.

"Guess I've been busy," her temporary housemate said with a disinterested shrug. "Ever since mom died a few years back, and I moved back in here when Dad took off to live in his fishing cabin, I guess it really doesn't feel much like home anymore. I do the bare minimum of upkeep, but that's about it."

On their way down a dark hall, he flipped on a weak overhead light, then kicked aside another stray blue sock.

"I'm sorry," Cassie said.

"No need to be. I never really had a Beaver Cleaver life to begin with. I mean, to outsiders, my folks made sure everything looked okay, but from the time I was ten, I knew things weren't. Here's your room," he said, stopping at the last door on the right.

He opened it, and upon her first glance, Cassie gasped.

"Noah, this—well, it's beyond words."

The large, pale yellow room wasn't just pretty—it was exquisite. An ornately carved dark walnut canopy bed dominated the west wall, flanked on both sides by matching side tables and eight-paned windows draped with the same yellow rose-patterned fabric as the bedspread and canopy.

Sunlight streamed in, bathing an intimate seating area on the south wall in a golden glow.

Tucked into a bay window was an upholstered window seat brimming with needlepoint pillows of flowers and quotes she couldn't wait to read. On the walls hung an interesting blend of antique plate collections and hats and black-and-white photos of long-gone ancestors.

Dotted here and there were colorful tapestry rugs, and blending nicely with the abundance of yellow were regal ferns on stands and delicate English ivies trailing over the rims of teacup planters and matching saucers.

Through an open door, Cassie glimpsed a white-tiled bathroom. Behind a closed door was, she assumed, a closet.

"I'm glad you like it," Noah said, yanking a dead leaf from the nearest fern. "This room meant a lot to my mother. From what little I've pieced together, she'd always wanted a daughter, but after three miscarriages—the last a close call with nearly dying—her doctor said no more. She had to have a hysterectomy, and Dad said she never recovered."

"Wow." Cassie swallowed hard. "I don't know what to say. That's awful."

Noah shrugged. "Water under the bridge. Anyway, I always viewed this room as her shrine to the little girl she wanted instead of me."

"Oh, Noah, you don't think that just because she wanted a girl means she loved you any less, do you?"

"I'll get your luggage, and the kids' toys and stuff, then show you the deck and my new gas grill."

"Noah, don't you want to—" *Talk?*

Too late, he'd already left the room.

Turning in a slow circle, Cassie once again drank in the space. Different from the rest of the house, this room held a faint lemony smell. Not a speck of dust rested on anything. Not on the dresser with its collection of silver-framed pictures of Noah as a boy. Not on any of the hardback classics lining a built-in bookshelf. Not even on the glass paperweights lounging on the seating area's coffee table, basking in the sun.

The room *was* a shrine.

But to who or what?

Noah's mother and the daughter she'd wanted? To Noah's lonely childhood—assuming he'd had one? To his ex-wife, or one of the women in the support group? Or to something more? Something Cassie sensed hiding deep inside him. Something all seventeen members of that goofy group also might have sensed, but hadn't identified.

Cassie, on the other hand, wondered if she might have accidentally stumbled across the answer.

Whether he knew it or not, could Noah, the breaker of hearts suffer from a broken one?

Having herself fallen victim to the very same malaise, Cassie figured she ought to be able to recognize the signs in others. Something she also recognized was the fact that no amount of talking or praying—or for that matter, dusting—would ever cure the disease. Maybe time would, but for her at least, not enough had passed yet for her to be able to tell.

Goose bumps dotted her arms.

Crossing them, she ran her hands up and down her shoulders, suppressing a shiver. For all the room's warmth, why was she suddenly so cold?

Chapter Four

"Thanks," Cassie said to Noah in the cereal aisle of Riverdale Grocery.

"For what?" he asked, snatching the box of fiber flakes from the top shelf and tossing it in their cart. He'd offered to push, but though she hadn't said anything to him, the day's activities were starting to take a toll. She was exhausted from her latest trip to the hospital to feed the babies and holding the cart gave her much-needed support. "Because if I were really and truly a good guy, I'd save you from eating this overpriced cat food in a pretty box."

She made a face.

"Seriously," she said, rounding the end cap piled high with Pop-Tarts to turn down the baby aisle. "Thank you. I'm not used to this damsel in distress role I seem to have fallen into. It seems like every time I turn around, caught yet again in another jam—this time unable to reach my favorite cereal—you gallop up on your trusty sheriff-steed to save me...I mean, us. Guess I need to start getting used to that, huh? The fact that I now have a family."

"Aw, shucks, ma'am," he said, pretending to whip off a cowboy hat while he deeply bowed. "'Twasn't nuthin'"

She swatted the top of his head with the store sale circular. "Just for a second, would you stop horsing around? I'm trying to be serious."

"But I'm tired of being serious," he complained. "We've done that for, like, the past two days, and it's starting to be a major drag."

"What's wrong with being serious? Without serious people, nothing would ever get done."

"Yeah," he said, "but things sure would get dull." They'd reached the baby toy section, and after snatching two of everything, he put it all in the cart.

"Noah!"

"What? The girls are going to need something to do. It's not like they're gonna be playing video games until they're at least six months old."

"Sure." Starting to remove all that he'd just put in, Cassie added, "And for the first month or so of those six, I've read they won't do much of anything besides eat, poop and sleep."

"So what you're essentially saying is that my home's about to be invaded by lazy, eating and pooping blobs?"

Crossing her arms, Cassie wanted to hold tight to the glare she'd shot his way, but then he cupped his hands around her elbows, drawing her close enough for her overwhelming awareness of him to gobble up all of her practical arguments, leaving her with nothing more to bicker about than how big to make her smile.

"You're a nut," she said, lingering in his strong hold. "Anyone ever tell you that?"

"All the time." He pressed a tender kiss to her forehead.

"What was that for?" she asked, surprising warmth flooding her weary body.

"For making this the most fun I've had at the grocery store in—"

"Noah." A stunning blonde rounded the corner with a towheaded baby and toddler in her cart—judging by the blue Baby Gap-wear, both boys. "You look as despicable as ever. But you…" she said to Cassie, her formerly icy expression transformed into a warm smile. "You must be the new lady in this rogue's life. I've heard so much about you."

"You have?" Cassie asked, eyebrows raised.

"Oh sure," the woman said with a graceful wave of French-manicured nails. "The story of how Noah delivered your babies right there on the side of the road is all anyone's talking about. Honey, you're a baby-making rock star!"

"Um, thanks. I think."

The gorgeous blonde—the only type Noah seemed to know—turned to him. "Well? Aren't you going to formally introduce us?"

Her toddler reached for the neatly lined jars of baby food. He had his eye on puréed plums, and while straining to get his chubby, pinching little fingers on one of those shiny jars, he'd stuck out his tongue.

"No, no, Brad," his mommy said. "Mustn't touch."

Noah snorted, then swooped the kid out of the cart, and straight over to his heart's desire, where he grabbed not one jar of plums, but two.

"Noah!" The woman barked. "Don't you know better than to just let kids have what they want?" She snatched the boy back. "Besides, those jars are glass. He could've been hurt."

Noah rolled his eyes.

"And good grief, where are your manners?" she asked, plopping her son back in the cart. "For heaven's sake, introduce us."

"Cass," he said, with a regal gesture, "Meet Jenny."

"Hi," Jenny gushed. "It's so nice to finally meet you. I'm official Number Four. Tiffany said she'd already welcomed you into our group."

Cassie turned to Noah, who'd pressed his lips tight.

The warm, caring friend she'd found in him just moments earlier had been replaced by a stone-faced man who looked every bit the part of a no-nonsense sheriff. Just an educated guess, but from the looks of his own cold expression, he'd had it with not only this woman, but the whole group!

"Um, nice to meet you," Cassie said, shaking Jenny's hand. "And who are these handsome fellows?"

The woman beamed at her adorable children. "Dylan is the baby, and Brad is the big one."

Brad was on his feet playing *Godzilla Smashes a Loaf of White Bread*. "Out! Out!"

Cassie held her breath waiting to see what catastrophe unfolded next. Maybe she'd been too hasty with that *adorable* assessment?

"Oh, look what you did, Noah. Now, you went and got him all wound up." After shooting Noah one more squinty-eyed glare, Jenny then turned to Cassie. "Hopefully, we'll meet again under more pleasant circumstances."

"Sure," Cassie said. "Bye."

Whoosh. They were gone.

"Good riddance," Noah muttered under his breath, reaching for a sack of newborn diapers.

"What was that?"

He shook his head.

"What's up with you and the members of that group? It's like they hate you."

Shrugging, he said, "Bunch of loonies, each and every one of them."

"Yet you dated them."

"Much to my everlasting regret."

"So what went wrong—seventeen times?"

"Oh, look," he said. "They've got teething biscuits. Guy down at the station brought 'em by accident one day in his lunch. We tried dunking 'em in coffee and found out they're not half-bad."

"Any particular reason you're changing the subject?" she asked, taking baby lotion, shampoo and oil from the shelf across the aisle.

His only answer was a sarcastic snort.

"Okay, I'll try another course." Hand on his shoulder, she gently turned him her way. "This time, let's go for the direct route. Why do those women have it in for you?''

Hardening his jaw, he said, ''What didn't you get the first time about my not-so-subtle stab at talking about something else?''

''Nothing, it's just that—''

''Look, I don't mean to come off like a world-class jerk here, but as long as we're going to be living together, let's get a couple of things straight. There are pretty much only two things I won't do for you—well, except for the obvious girlie stuff like painting your toenails or braiding your hair. Assuming we lump all the rest of that female stuff together, and then put it aside, there are only two other things I won't do.''

''Okay. Let's hear them.''

''One. I refuse to eat that fiber crap you just put in the cart—or any other incarnation thereof.''

''Duly noted,'' she said with a curt nod, not bothering trying to hide the mischievous twinkle in her eyes. ''And number two on your list of won'ts?''

''I won't ever want to discuss that stupid, freakin' support group.''

''Gotcha. Roger and out.''

When she wheeled on down to the end of the aisle without so much as glancing his way, he jogged in front of the cart and brought her to a speedy halt. ''You think this is funny?''

''Your list?''

''Shoot, yeah, my list.''

Grinning, she said, ''Noah, sweetie, it's not just funny, but downright hilarious.''

He was back to hardening his jaw.

"Aw, don't go getting mad. You just have to look at it from my perspective."

"What's that?"

"Well, for a guy who supposedly doesn't want to even have the almighty words *support group* mentioned in his presence, you sure are all hot and bothered about it."

"Your point being?"

"Well, if this group truly doesn't matter to you, why are you so wound up?" She curled her hand around his forearm, squeezing his tight muscles. "See? You're all tense." Not to mention rock-hard sexy.

"I can't help it. They get to me, all right?" Raking his fingers through his hair, Noah looked away from her piercing green gaze to a nice, safe shelf stacked with paper towels. "Who knows why. They just do."

"Ah, finally," she said, massaging his forearm, shooting all manner of unwelcome questions through his already confused brain. Questions like, what would it feel like were she to keep that massage going all the way up to his aching shoulders and neck? And how did she fit so much strength into her petite little frame? "We're starting to see some glimmer of truth behind all your blustery bravado."

"You think all of this is an act?"

"No. Just that you're hiding your true feelings."

"What feelings? According to that crew, I'm not in possession of a single, solitary one."

"Bull. You wanna know what I think your trouble is?"

"Please, do tell."

"I think if anything, you care too much."

"I'M SORRY, OKAY?" Cassie put her hand on Noah's shoulder, but he flinched away. They stood at his kitchen counter, unpacking groceries, and he hadn't uttered more than a grunt since she'd made the apparently unfortunate decision of speaking her mind.

"You've got nothing to be sorry for," he said, slamming her box of fiber flakes onto the tile.

"Then why are you all bent out of shape?"

"Who said I was?"

"This is nuts," she said, slamming her own carton of tofu to the counter beside her vase brimming with fragrant yellow roses—the roses Noah had given her. His were the only flowers she'd kept. All of the rest she'd given to patients in the geriatric wing. But these—these she couldn't bear to part with. Now that he was in such a grouchy mood, she thought the notion of them being extra special because he'd given them to her was silly and sentimental. "I'd be better off camped at the hospital."

Noah sighed, pulled her into a hug. "I'm the one who should be sorry," he said into her hair. "Those women—they make me crazy. It's like I go through some freaky Dr. Jekyll thing whenever one of them comes around."

"But why?" she asked, pulling back to look into his eyes. "I mean, if you broke up with them, then it should be over."

"That's just it," he said with a laugh, leaving her

to slip a sack of tomatoes into the vegetable bin of the fridge. "When things went south, they all broke up with me."

"Then why do they still seem so bitter?"

"You tell me. 'Cause from where I'm standing, I was the injured party."

"What'd they do?"

"Just dumped me."

"Without warning?"

"Well..."

"Oh boy, here it comes." She grinned on her way to the oak kitchen table that filled a windowed nook. Golden evening sun slanted through the paned windows, painting the room with a honeyed glow. She drew out one of the roomy chairs, plopped herself onto the cheerful gingham seat cushion, then slipped off her shoes. Only after she'd put her feet up on the chair beside her did she say, "All right. Carry on."

"You sure you're comfy?" he asked, eyeing the remaining three sacks of food still needing to be put away.

"Completely."

"Great." He shot her an easy grin. "So, anyway, where were we?"

"You were just about to tell me what *eee-vil* manthing you did to make these beautiful, talented women run in horror."

"Right. Okay, so basically, pretty much the only thing I did was refuse to get hitched. Geez, how much of this green stuff did you buy?" he asked, holding bunches of radicchio, butter-leaf and purple-leaf lettuce.

"Hey! Watch it, buddy! That stuff bruises easily."

"Unlike me?"

"You said it."

He stuffed her lettuce into the already cramped veggie bin, but Cassie let his lettuce-battering go unpunished, sensing he might be on the verge of actually spilling his feelings.

"You refused to marry them, huh?"

"That's pretty much it."

"Were they pregnant? Because if so, then that pretty much makes you despicable."

He shot her a dirty look. "No, they weren't pregnant. Geez, what kind of a two-headed monster do you take me for?"

"Hey, I had to ask."

"Well, just so we're clear on this—no, again. When I make a commitment, by God, I stick to it."

"So why wouldn't you commit to any of these women? I mean, when two people are really into each other, marriage is the next logical step, don't you think?"

"Remember that list of unmentionables I gave you back at the store?"

"Yes."

"Let's add a third. As for the whole tying the knot thing…" He shook his head. "Let's not go there."

Nodding, attempting to lean forward to rub her aching feet, but not quite making it, she said, "Believe me, I can relate. One marriage is way more than I needed to teach me I never want to be anywhere near that institution again.''

He abandoned the groceries to lift her feet, then rest them on his lap when he sat in the chair opposite her. Rubbing them with hypnotically strong strokes, he said, ''You've been burned, too, huh?''

''Wait a minute, how'd we go from you to me? I still haven't heard your sad saga—*ooh, yes*,'' she said, closing her eyes as he deepened his strokes through her arches. ''Lord, you're good at this.''

''You think this is good, you should see me work my magic with a barbecue grill.''

''Yeah, yeah, we'll get to that later. For now, just keep rubbing.''

''Demanding little thing, aren't you?''

''Hey, I figure if you don't ask for what you want, nobody else is going to do it for you.''

''True,'' he said with a grimace.

''So? Let's hear it. Who broke your heart?''

He groaned. ''Do we really have to get into this now? I mean, if you've been through the whole divorce thing, too, then—''

''I'm not divorced,'' she said.

''Then what happened? This creep hit the road once he found out you were pregnant?''

Swallowing hard, trying to be glib on the subject she could still barely think of without tears filling her eyes, she said. ''My babies' father died.''

''Oh, geez…'' Noah stopped rubbing her toes to cup

them. "I'm sorry. Some folks—mainly of the female persuasion—say I have a genuine knack for being an insensitive jerk. Guess they would be right."

"Believe me, it was my husband who was the jerk." Smiling through tears she hastily wiped away, she said, "And come to think of it, just like he's better off dead, we're probably better off just getting back to unloading the groceries."

After slipping her feet off his lap, Cassie started to stand, but warm, strong hands on her shoulders urged her back down. "Let me do the rest," he said. "You go do whatever it is you women do."

"I'm not an invalid, you know."

"Yes, I know, which is why I'll let you do all the work you want—tomorrow. Now, go on, rest up before our last trip to feed those munchkins of ours."

She was halfway to the arch leading to the hall when she turned back. "Don't you mean munchkins of mine?"

"Huh?" He stashed a box of rice in a cabinet.

"The babies."

"Yeah? What about them?"

"You said they were ours."

"I did?"

"Never mind," she said, hand to her forehead. "I must've just heard you wrong. Anyway, thanks for taking me to the store, and for… Well, you know."

"You're welcome," he said, toppling her heart with the potency of his handsome grin.

AT THE HOSPITAL later that night Noah caught sight of Cass breastfeeding Noelle through a missing slat in the nursery's shades. He turned away out of respect. But damned if he didn't want to watch.

There was nothing sexual about the scene, just bone-deep intimacy.

The kind of intimacy Cass should have been sharing with her husband—not some guy she'd picked up on the side of the road.

Shoot, her now-deceased spouse couldn't have been all that bad. At least he had married her. After what Darla had put him through, Noah knew he'd never get hitched again. Which was a real shame, seeing how at the moment, he could think of nothing more pleasant than kicking back on a weeknight and witnessing such an act of motherly love.

Now that kind of bonding—that would be cool.

But seeing how he wasn't about to have kids without giving them his name, and he'd already established the fact that he'd never marry again, looked like this was as close as he'd be getting to fatherhood.

"Hey, Noah. How's Cassie been feeling?"

His stomach sank.

Nurse Helen.

Approaching fast.

"She's, ah, been fine," he said, tucking his hands in his pockets. "You know, the usual tiredness."

Her expression all business, she nodded. "Sure, that's to be expected."

"I guess so."

He'd forgotten how pretty Helen was, and what a fun time they used to have together. What had gone wrong? They used to talk for hours, and now, here they stood in this long, sterile hall, neither of them knowing what to say.

"Well… Good night." She gave him a half wave, before heading toward the nurse's station.

"'Night." Who knew what had gotten into him to then shout, "Hey, Helen! Wait!"

"What?" she asked when he'd caught up.

"I, ah, have something I'd like to ask."

"Okay."

"Why did the two of us break up?"

Clutching a metal-bound chart to her chest, she rolled her eyes.

"What? It's a legitimate question."

"It's also ancient history."

"So? Having all that time to think it over ought to have given you a lot clearer perspective."

"Oh, I'm not rolling my eyes because of any lack of perspective, Noah Wheeler, but out of surprise. Even you can't be so blind that you'd have to ask."

Hardening his jaw, staring off at the dark window down the hall rather than at her annoyed expression, he said, "Yeah, well, humor me. Sometimes even the blind need a helping hand now and then."

Three rooms down, a patient call light went on.

"I have to get that," she said.

"I'll be here when you get back."

''No, Noah. You won't, because the two of us have nothing more to say.''

Stunned by the chill behind her words, Noah looked at his feet while she took off for the patient's room.

That couldn't have gone any worse.

But then what the hell kind of answer had he been after anyway? He already knew they'd broken up because she'd wanted the whole church wedding thing with like eight pink bridesmaids and a wedding cake the size of a freaking Volkswagen! And all he'd wanted was to—

''Ready?''

He looked up to see Cass looking small and scared. Her big green eyes shone with tears, and all of a sudden Helen and her arctic chill no longer existed, because Cass not only needed him, she appreciated him. And didn't go off on him after all he'd done was ask one innocent little question.

''What's wrong?'' he asked, slipping his arm about her shoulders to lead her toward the elevator.

''I'm such a big baby,'' she said, sniffling while shaking her head.

''So? Tell me anyway.'' He pressed the down button, and the doors opened with a ding.

Stepping into the car, with his arm still around her, she said, ''It's just that earlier today, Doctor Joe said the babies might be able to come home tomorrow morning, but the nurse just told me that to be on the safe side, he'd like them to stay one more full day.''

''What's so tragic about that?''

"N-nothing," she said, still sniffling. "It's just that I wanted to get them home. You know, get them settled into their nest, and now, here we are, still imposing on you. And I—"

"Shh…" He pulled her into a hug, hating himself for loving the way she felt in his arms. He'd never held a woman so small. So delicate, yet so strong. "Everything's gonna be okay. Before you know it, those babies'll be home squalling their eyeballs out, and then you'll wish they were back in the hospital."

"You think?" she asked, peering up at him with her impossibly big green eyes.

"Oh, yeah. Heck, yeah. I'm pretty sure I've even read it in a training manual at work."

"You did not, you big fibber." She landed a swat to his chest, only it wasn't really a swat, but more of a caress, and then he was pulling her close again, and swearing if she didn't stop staring at him that way his heart would pound right out of his chest.

He had to kiss her. Only he wasn't sure how to go about coming in for a landing. And the timing was all wrong, and he couldn't even think with her staring up at him that way. Like he was some kind of protector when in actuality, he was more of a big bad wolf, trying to steal nookie off a poor, defenseless single mom!

Ding.

The elevator doors swished open, and the moment was gone.

Taking her small hand in his big one, though, he

sadly realized that while the moment might be gone, the feelings weren't. And that was bad. Because good guys who knew full well they had no intention of ever getting hitched sure as hell didn't put the moves on single moms.

Not cool.

At all.

So where did that leave him? With one helluva a rocket in his pocket destined to land with a thud.

Chapter Five

"Hey there, stranger!" Brenda called out the next afternoon as Noah led Cassie into the burger joint.

As usual around lunchtime, the place was packed.

Though a country ballad blared from the jukebox, the din of conversation and the occasional guffaw rose above the tune. There wasn't a table to be had save for one, and good thing for him, Brenda always kept her best back booth reserved for the sheriff, claiming that it made good financial sense to stay on the right side of the law.

Cass had long since traded her sexy pj's for an equally disturbing little black dress more suited to some fancy cocktail party than to fitting in with this rowdy bunch. Still, Noah couldn't help but straighten his shoulders with pride seeing all of the admiring, good old boy glances aimed her way.

"Hey yourself, Bren," he said. "How about bringing us two of my usual?"

"What's that?" Cassie asked over her shoulder.

"It's a surprise. But I promise, you'll like it."

Brenda asked, "You havin' a Coke day or malt day, Sheriff?"

Catching a glimpse of Cassie's ripe behind a few steps in front of him, Noah swallowed hard before hollering, "Malt!"

"Will do!"

"Sheriff." Floyd Hopkins spun on his black vinyl stool to glare. "Mind tellin' me why that thug over there isn't having lunch behind bars?"

Without a glance in the boy's direction, Noah knew full well who Floyd was talking about. Zane McNally. Riverdale's self-appointed bad boy who just couldn't seem to get the hint that either he change his ways, or he was headed for juvie hell.

In the booth two places down from him sat the same trio of gigglers Noah had seen the last time he'd been at Brenda's. They were neatly dressed, nice-looking girls. Good girls, with undoubtedly good grades. Seeing how he wasn't familiar with them, he was guessing they'd just moved into that fancy new subdivision south of town. Anyway, they'd do well to steer clear of Zane.

Noah said, "As much as I wish I could tell you different, Floyd, I got nothin' to charge Zane on."

"Whaddoyou mean? He was trespassin' on my property just last night and I wanna press charges. It's because of him and his gang of thugs that that momma Hereford of mine miscarried."

"Now, Floyd, you don't have any—"

"You get those boys, Sheriff—'specially that McNally kid. Been trouble since the day he was born."

"I'll do my best, Floyd."

"Yeah, well, you'd better do a damned sight more than that, or I'll make it my life's mission to see to it you never win another campaign."

Noah met the man's squinty-eyed gaze with a challenge of his own that told Floyd to keep out of his business. Noah wasn't good at a lot of things, but he did know the law. Granted, much of it he'd learned from being on the wrong side of it, but that was a whole other story. One he'd need a couple dozen beers instead of malts to feel like getting into.

"Wow," Cass said, eyeing Noah as he slid into the opposite side of the booth. "What was that all about? I couldn't hear any of it, but for a second there, every eye in the room was on you."

Noah shrugged, then snatched one of the plastic covered menus Brenda stashed behind the napkin holder, more to avoid Cass's eyes than because he was having doubts about what he'd ordered.

"Seriously, that guy has it in for you. His daughter isn't a member of the infamous support group, is she?"

"Drop it."

"Ooh, hit a sore spot, did I? Okay, let's see if I can piece this scenario together without your help. You dated Cindy Sue for a whole year before she started talking china patterns and you were forced to break her heart?"

Somehow holding his fury in check, Noah glared at the menu. Patty melt. He'd have to try that. The hoagie sounded good, too.

"Mmm, I must be getting close, but haven't yet hit

it on the dot. I know you're too noble to get a girl pregnant and run, so maybe you just let things get a little too far past the china zone? Maybe she was already checking out silverware patterns, too? And talking towel colors and—''

''Enough!'' Noah growled, glancing over his shoulder to see if any of his not-so-adoring fans were taking this in. Thankfully, they all seemed pretty focused on their burgers. ''Where'd this nasty streak come from, Cass?''

''What do you mean?'' she asked with an innocent smile.

''All this badgering. Even if there was a *Cindy Sue,* why do you care?''

''Maybe because I've been hurt by one of your kind. Bad.''

''One of my kind? We've had some fun messing around, Cass, but beyond that—you don't even know me.''

Not budging from the challenge in Noah's gaze, she raised her chin. ''Seeing the anger in that man's eyes, Noah, sadly yes, I'm afraid I do know you. So far, all of the other women in this group who I've met have turned out fine. They're happily married with babies and comfy homes, but this one. This one, I can tell just by the fire in her father's eyes that she still isn't over you. Maybe she never will be.''

Giving her a good, long stare, Noah clapped her a sarcastic round of applause. ''Congratulations. Boy, you really nailed it that time.''

''But you don't feel bad?''

"Why should I?"

She swallowed hard, and if only for an instant, he'd have sworn he'd glimpsed pain crossing her eyes. "Because like I said, I've been in this girl's place, and heartache isn't fun."

"And you automatically assume I'm to blame? That all guys are to blame?" That it'd been his fault when Darla ran out on him after just six months because he'd busted his knee? That just as soon as she'd heard his pro-football contract with the Dallas Cowboys had been ever-so-politely pulled, that she'd been out of his life faster than Zane leaving the scene of his latest crime? And it was his fault that Floyd couldn't see what a mistake it'd be to just lock Zane up without at least giving him a chance to turn his life around? Shoot, if now retired Sheriff Bowles hadn't given Noah a second chance all those years ago, who knew where his life would've headed? Probably straight down the toilet.

"Well?" Cass asked. "I can't wait to hear how no guy has ever done wrong."

Running his fingers through his hair, Noah said, "I've gotta get out of here."

"Oh sure—run. That's just great."

"Enjoy your lunch," he said. "I'll tell Brenda to put it on my tab. The hospital's just around the corner—barely even half a block. I'll pick you up there in a couple hours."

"Noah, wait. I—"

Without turning back, Noah stopped by the register.

"Hey, Bren, could you please have Yancie drop my meal by the station?"

"Sure, but—"

"Thanks. Gotta run."

HANDS ON HER HIPS, Brenda looked to the teensy red-head in the rear booth who was craning her neck to get a better view of the sheriff's retreating backside. Lovely as his tight buns were, the sudden pallor of that prissy missy's perfect complexion told Brenda that a whole lot more was going on here than Noah having been pulled away to answer a call.

That cantankerous old Floyd had already gone off on him. And then she felt sure the sheriff would still be upset over Kelsey's wedding. And there was out of control Zane, sitting pretty as you please in a window booth when everyone knew he should've been in third-period English. And now, obviously, this woman had said something to land Noah in a snit—and after the poor man had spent so much time caring for *her* babies!

Loading *Red's* share of their meal onto a yellow plastic tray, Brenda headed that way. By golly, if she had said something to upset Noah, she'd darned well pay for it. That boy had been through more than his fair share of heartache.

"You ought to be full well ashamed of yourself," Brenda said, slamming the tray onto the woman's table.

"Excuse me?" Red gave her a funny look.

Brenda wasn't putting up with a second of this tart's

sass. Gathering the generous side fabric of her orange muumuu, she snorted before sliding into Noah's empty seat.

"There's no excusing the likes of you," she railed, rattling off her list of everything Noah must have on his mind. "Making matters even worse, is that old Floyd over there doesn't have a clue just how torn poor Noah is over this whole mess with Zane. Shoot, the man's older than God, you'd think he'd remember what a tough time of it Noah himself had had before he turned his life around."

"So that man—Floyd—wasn't yelling at Noah for breaking his daughter's heart?" Red looked like she was two breaths from barfing. She better make it to the bathroom. Barfing was always bad for business!

"Where on earth did you get a crazy idea like that?" Brenda asked. "Floyd never even had a wife—let alone kids—praise be."

"Oh."

"Well? You gonna eat?"

"Thanks, but I'm not really all that hungry." Red slid out of the booth, left a twenty on the table, then darted out of the room and into the sunshine-flooded spring day.

Eyeing Red, wishing her rail-thin hips straight onto the nearest skinny person island, Brenda snatched up her untouched double cheeseburger and took a big bite. No sense in lettin' good food go to waste!

CASSIE, having wound her way down a series of brightly lit halls lined with FBI Wanted posters, tentatively knocked on the door she'd been directed to by the balding man staffing the front desk of Riverdale's sheriff's department. Even from here, she still heard elevator music from the Martha Stewart tape the man had been watching while filing.

"Go away!" barked a muffled voice that sounded an awful lot like Noah's.

An eye-level plaque on the wall beside the door read Sheriff Noah Wheeler, so she assumed she was in the right place.

Drawn to the plaque, to his name, she skimmed her fingertips along the engraved black letters, wishing that back there at the restaurant she'd kept her big, betrayed and still bitter mouth shut.

Seeing how she hadn't, she knocked again.

"What?!"

"Noah… It's me."

"If *me* means a know-it-all redhead going by the name of Cassie, I'll see you later at the hospital."

Taking that as an invitation, Cassie opened his office door, finding him seated behind a battered metal desk. Behind him were two tall windows with four dead begonias lining the sills. Stacks of manila folders covered every flat surface—including the seats of two brown plastic guest chairs. "Hi."

"I thought I told you to—"

"I'm sorry," she said in the hopes of stealing his thunder. "Back at the restaurant—everything I said. I was completely out of line, and I'm sorry."

Pen still in hand, he looked up. "Brenda's is a burger joint—not a restaurant."

"O-okay. I'm sorry for getting that wrong, too."

"And for the record, you *were* out of line."

"I know. Brenda told me."

He shot her a grin. "In that case, you have my condolences."

"She was pretty rough on me, but I can't say I didn't have it coming."

He shrugged. "I could've steered you down the right trail."

"Knowing all you've done for me and the babies, I should've never gone down the wrong trail. I should've trusted you, Noah, and I'm sorry."

"Sheriff?" Another knock sounded on the now open door. The bald man who'd directed Cassie to Noah's office wagged a grease-splotched bag and paper cup. "Yancie just dropped this by."

"Thanks," Noah said, leaving his chair to meet the man halfway across the room.

"Sure thing."

The man left, and Noah set the bag and cup on the shortest of the piles on his desk, then started clearing the guest chair of its paper burden.

"Don't," Cassie said. "You go ahead and eat. I'll grab something at the hospital."

"You didn't eat at Brenda's?"

Swallowing hard, remembering the dark look on Noah's usually serene face, she shook her head.

"Then I'll share."

"Noah, I—"

"What?" he said with a bold wink. "Don't tell me

you're afraid to share a straw? I promise I don't have cooties.''

She reddened. In truth, she hadn't even considered the shared straw factor since her mind was still on worrying what she'd do if their fingers happened to touch in the Tater Tot bag!

''I know you don't have cooties,'' she said.

''Then what are you afraid of?'' He'd gone back to clearing the chair, but he'd grabbed too many files at once, and the remaining pile started to topple.

She lurched for it just as he did, but in the end both of them were too late, and the whole pile oozed like a runaway mudslide onto the beige vinyl floor. Suppressing a giggle at the mess that was so horrible it landed in the category of either laugh about it or cry, she said, ''That was what I was afraid of.''

Jaw tight, he nodded. ''Me, too.''

''Well, then. Guess I should get going.''

''And leave me with this mess?''

Cassie said, ''Ginnie, my receptionist, would be the first to tell you, I've never been all that good at filing.''

''That's no excuse.''

''Really,'' she argued. ''I even have to sing the alphabet every time to remember if *H* comes before or after *G*. And *I?* I'm clueless when it comes to *I*.''

''In that case,'' he said, wagging the sack of food, ''we'll just take this show on the road.''

TEN MINUTES LATER, Cassie sat with Noah outside in glorious sun.

The sheriff's office courtyard looked all but abandoned with tall weeds, a lone pouting pine, and a concrete picnic table that had definitely seen better days. Still, as Cassie leaned her head back and closed her eyes, drinking in the warm sun, she realized that combined with such pleasant company, even such a dismal spot couldn't hide spring's glory.

Not a breath of breeze stirred the not-too-cold, not-too-hot air ripe with the scents of far-off budding maples and oaks and dogwoods. Hidden away as they were, Cassie mused that here in this secret garden, they might as well have been the only two people on earth—at least until the occasional broken muffler or honked horn brought reality crashing back in.

"Damn," Noah said, eyeing a mound of paper cups and wadded papers that'd huddled into the courtyard's shadowed north corner. "Guess it's been a while since anyone's been out here."

"That's understandable. Judging by the mountains of files in your office, I'm sure you don't have a lot of time for gardening."

"True, but this is—well, anyway. Let's eat."

"Sure. You go first," she said while he unwrapped the burger's greasy foil.

"Oh no," he said. "I know this look. What's the matter now?"

"Nothing."

"Is it the crappy ambiance?"

"Not at all." She stared intently at her lap.

"The company?"

Shyly glancing up, she said, "You know that's not it."

"Ahh…" A trickle of grease slid down his thumb and he licked it off. "Little Miss Health Food's probably never seen a burger quite like this." He sunk his teeth in for a juicy bite, closing his eyes in pure, burger bliss. "Damn, that Brenda knows how to make a burger."

"You are so bad! Do you have any idea how much cholesterol that thing must have?"

"Nope. And I don't care, either." He held the burger out to her. "Here. See for yourself."

"That's okay," she said, shaking her head. "I'll grab a yogurt at the hospital snack bar."

"I insist."

"Why?"

"Because double cheeseburgers are a food of the gods. You mustn't risk offending them."

"I'll take my chances," Cassie said. "I've been quite safe for the past twenty-seven years without ever having tasted one. Surely I can go at least a few minutes more."

"Never?" He raised his eyebrows.

"What?"

"Had a cheeseburger?"

"Well, of course." She paused a moment. "I think. I mean, surely at one point or another, but—is this a problem for you? The fact that maybe I haven't had a cheeseburger?"

A bee buzzed off the head of a dandelion to dive-bomb Cassie's hair.

"See?" Noah said, all smiles when the creature finally went on his way. "I told you the burger gods were gonna be royally ticked."

"Oh, all right," Cassie said. "Give me a bite."

She reached for it, but he said, "Not so fast. A moment like this must be handled with a certain amount of finesse."

When she rolled her eyes, the bee came buzzing back.

Chapter Six

Eyeing the bee buzzing Cassie's head, Noah's grin grew broader than ever.

"Oh, get on with it," she said.

Meeting her gaze, burger between both hands, he raised it to her lips.

Cassie steeled herself for the worst.

Eyes closed, she bit down, trying not to think about the fact that Noah's strong teeth and firm lips had only moments earlier been where hers were about to go. Hands on his wrists, she took her first damning bite, and like Eve succumbing to her first delicious bite of apple, Cassie was lost in juicy, exhilarating sin!

"Well?" he asked once she opened her eyes, sitting back to watch the view.

She shrugged. "Um, it was okay." *Okay?! Oh my God, it was fantastic! Heaven! Better than sex! Granted, it'd been a while since she'd experienced the joys of the latter, but—*

"Cass? Got anything you'd like to confess?"

"Um, about what?"

"You know…"

"I already told you I was sorry for jumping to conclusions back at Brenda's."

"Ooh, you're a slippery one. As you're usually only too happy to point out, I've known a few women in my life, and the look I just saw cross your face was one of pure bliss. You're in love, Ms. Cassie Tremont. And not with me, or even Brad Pitt! You're in love with a double cheeseburger with extra mayo and pickles!"

"Am not!" she said, grabbing him by his wrists again to snag another bite.

"Then what was that?"

"You don't think I want that bee coming back, do you?"

Grinning, he took another bite himself then offered her a drink of the malt—which she wholeheartedly accepted.

After they spent a few minutes eating in companionable silence, she said, "Brenda told me that after I went to bed last night, you went to work."

He shrugged.

To which she nudged him with her shoulder. "That's a bad habit of yours, you know?"

"What?"

"All of this shrugging instead of answering."

He started to shrug again, then shot her a sheepish grin.

"See?"

"I'm pleading the Fifth."

"Yeah, well, what you ought to plead is exhaustion."

He started to shrug, but then said, "I'm used to it."

"You shouldn't be. Keeping those kinds of hours is unhealthy."

"That mean you care?"

"About your health? Yes."

"I'm flattered."

"You should be concerned. Especially since this regular burger feast of yours isn't exactly a grilled salmon with steamed veggies platter."

He made a face. "Thank God."

CONTENT IN a hospital rocking chair, nursing Hope, smoothing her hand over her baby girl's soft strawberry-blond curls, Cassie's thoughts drifted like lazy spring clouds. From cheeseburgers to malts to a handsome sheriff with warm brown eyes and a soul-melting grin.

"Oh, baby…" she said to Hope. "He's such a mystery."

The more time Cassie spent with him, the less she knew.

Who was this Zane kid he was determined to save—even at the expense of his job? And who was this Kelsey woman he was supposedly so broken up over? Those two biggies barely scratched the surface of what she'd like to know.

Like what'd happened between him and his former wife? And how come every time she mentioned *The Support Group,* they always ended up in an argument?

The biggest mystery of all was why she cared.

In a few days, she and the babies would be happily

back in Little Rock. Back in their modern home with its soaring white walls and miles of view. Back at the business she'd worked years to get to its current level of success.

All of this—Noah, his women and his troubles with this delinquent named Zane—none of it should even matter. She had her own troubles. Like calling her best friend and assistant, Chloe, and having her order the Becketts a new marble countertop to replace the one that'd been cracked in shipping. And dealing with the Newton's know-it-all architect who'd designed such a complex space that there wasn't a single solitary wall in the whole house long enough to display even one of their priceless French armoires—let alone their entire collection of fifteen!

And what about that other problem, Cassie? The one about your husband having shattered everything you've ever held sacred and true? When are you going to deal with that?

Swallowing hard, tracing the outline of Hope's pale brow, Cassie decided on tomorrow.

Tomorrow she'd think about all of her worries.

In the meantime, she had another baby to feed, and then another man. A better man who went by the name of Noah Wheeler who'd had nothing but junk food to eat for who knew how long. But tonight, all of that was going to change when she made him a super healthy thank-you feast!

"WHAT'S THE NAME of this again?" Noah asked from his seat at the kitchen table, trying not to blanch at the stringy, clingy, goopy mess on his plate that looked suspiciously like albino worms.

"Tofu linguini alfredo with bean sprouts. Good, huh?"

Thankfully, since Noah was still chewing the bite he'd just taken, she seemed satisfied with a nod as opposed to rave reviews. That afternoon, while he'd fitfully napped before his shift, he'd dreamed the smells drifting into his bedroom had been from normal foods like onions and chicken, but now he knew different! What she'd really been concocting was poison!

Oh well, however bad the food might be, at least the company was tasty.

And with the early evening sun slanting through the kitchen nook's windows, bathing Cass in a golden glow, Noah didn't think he'd ever seen her look more pretty. Not that he had that big of a catalogue of memories with her to look back on, but still, she looked great. He'd have told her so, but somehow to give voice to such a thing didn't seem appropriate. After all, he had sort of taken her and her little family under his protective wings, and the last thing he wanted was to act like some kind of lecher out to take advantage of her in her vulnerable condition.

"Noah?"

"Yeah?" He took a long swig of the herbal iced tea she'd brewed. While it wasn't as sweet as he usually liked, at least it was drinkable. As for the stringy white stuff on his plate…

"About this afternoon," Cassie said. "At Brenda's?"

"What of it?" He forced down another bite, seriously considering signing up for one of those reality shows, 'cause shoot, if he could choke down this muck, he could darn well eat anything!

"Well." She pressed her napkin to her lips, set it beside her plate.

Hey! No fair her quitting. She still had half a plate to go!

"I just want you to know again how sorry I am for telling you off like that—you know, jumping to conclusions."

He shrugged.

"No, I know that's your way of casually declaring it doesn't matter, but it does. When I was with the girls, I realized something."

Never had he been more grateful to set down his fork and listen.

"The reason I've been so snippy about this support group that I've supposedly been inducted into is because my husband hurt me pretty badly. As a result, I guess I've lumped you—and all men, for that matter—into a category of heartbreakers, when according to Brenda, in your case, at least, that couldn't be further from the truth."

"Brenda's mouth is as big as her burgers," he said with a sarcastic snort.

"Yeah, well, in this case, maybe that's a good thing. She opened my eyes not just to you, but myself."

Elbows planted on the table, Noah asked, "Just what did this husband of yours do?"

While they cleared the table and she filled his

mother's kettle with water for hot herbal tea, Cassie told him her sad tale, and by the end, if Tom hadn't already been dead, Noah would have hunted down the bastard himself.

Spotting a lone tear sliding down her cheek, Noah left his perch on one of the counter stools to pull her into his arms, and while she had a good cry and the teapot wailed, he held her and rocked her and damned all men, but most especially himself for being so hypersensitive about his own bad luck with women that he hadn't stopped to consider the fact that probably a helluva lot more women get hurt by men than the other way around.

"I should turn off the water," she said with a brave sniffle, palms warming his chest.

"Screw the water."

"But…"

Careful, oh so careful, he skimmed fiery hair back from her forehead, revealing not just the whole of her face, but the whole of her pain.

At that moment, gazing into the hurt shading her luminous green eyes, he wished for the power to fix her broken heart. Just as he'd wished for the power to fix Zane, and that woman who'd died in his arms all those years ago on the side of Blue Springs Road. And even further back, how he'd wished for the power to fix his parents' and his own marriages.

For a few precious moments, Cass melted against him, absorbing his strength. And in her needing him, he felt somehow whole. Better. But then she tensed and gently withdrew.

"Um, let's leave the dishes for in the morning," she said, gazing at the sink. "I'm beat."

"Sure," he said with a wobbly nod, wondering what had just happened, yet knowing. He'd just put himself out there only to be pushed away. Which was cool. Great, actually, 'cause he was in no frame of mind to add this woman to the top of his already lengthy list of troubles.

She stood there looking fragile and alone, neither of them saying a word, the steady drip of the kitchen-sink faucet the only sound save for the pounding of his heart.

"Yeah," he finally said, if only to mask the awkward silence. "Guess I should try getting a couple hours shut-eye, too."

"What time do you go in?"

"Eleven."

"I thought most sheriffs let their deputies handle the graveyard shift?"

"They do." *But I'm not most sheriffs, and 'round here, lately most of the action has been going down at night. And if I'm ever going to have a chance of fixing Zane, I'm going to need a front row seat to his latest stunt.*

"Okay, then, I guess this is good night."

He made the mistake of glancing at her lips. Full, soft, begging-to-be-kissed lips that caused all manner of below-the-belt distress.

Geez, what kind of lightweight had he become? Getting a woody just admiring a woman's lips? "Yeah.

Good night. You ah, go on ahead. I'll close the place down.''

''You sure? Because if you want, I can help.'' She did the cutest little flip with her hands, causing her severe black dress to pull at her full breasts—causing a not-so-innocent pang in him.

For just that moment, she'd looked soft. Not like the capable career woman he knew her to be, but like someone who might not only need him, but want him.

He swallowed hard.

Heck, yeah, he was sure.

Sure that if she didn't get out of his sight in the next three seconds, he'd pull her into his arms for a kiss that'd leave her not having a good night, but a frustrated one—just like the one he knew he'd be having! ''Yeah. I'm sure.''

''All right, then. Good night.''

''Good night.''

''Oh—and Noah?''

''Uh-huh?'' When she said his name, a sliver of her pink tongue escaped those sexy lips. Lips he had no business even looking at, let alone thinking of in bedroom terminology.

''The doctor said the babies should be able to leave tomorrow.''

''That's, ah, great.'' Because that meant she'd be leaving, too.

In the words of Briggs's each and every Martha Stewart tape…Cass and her whole irresistible crew hitting the road was *a good thing*.

"Hey, Sheriff?" Jimmy asked that evening in the tomb-quiet sheriff's office lobby just as Noah was heading out on patrol.

"Yeah?" Noah's stomach hurt from that supposedly healthy meal. Even worse was his frustration from time spent trying to make Cass smile—and failing. In the end, it'd been a relief tucking her into bed—well, if saying good-night in the kitchen even counted as tucking. He was tired, too—damn tired, he thought, gripping the back of one of the rickety waiting area chairs.

His only saving grace was that with Cass's girls being sprung from the hospital in the morning, he'd soon be released from the unexpected sense of responsibility he felt for the lot of them.

"So then that'd be cool with you?" Jimmy asked in the high-pitched whine he used whenever asking something he already knew the answer to.

"Huh? What'd be cool?"

"You already said it would. No take-backs now."

Noah hardened his jaw. "This isn't junior high, James. Repeat the question. I'm still not caught up on my beauty sleep."

"I was just gonna ask if you wanted me to take Cassie's car out on patrol tonight? You know—kind of use it as a decoy? No one in a million years would ever guess it was me behind the wheel."

"You got that right," Noah said with a snort on his way out the door.

"Then you think it's a good idea?"

''No,'' he said, already outside, jangling keys in hand. ''But hey, gotta give you brownie points for trying.''

AN HOUR LATER, Noah was on his third cup of the stale black coffee Brenda had put in a thermos for him, and had just pulled onto the King Road lookout point, hoping that since Zane hadn't been home when Noah had driven by there, at least from up here he'd have a great view of most of the kid's favorite haunts.

This time of night—or he guessed that it was now morning—he was usually up here hassling drunk teens who were getting it on in the back seat of their mom and dads' sedans. But tonight, Noah was on his own with the chirping crickets and *her*. Cass. Her laugh so addictive that even in the short time he'd known her, it'd become like a drug he could never seem to get enough of. Those eyes he could lose himself in if she gave him the slightest invitation. That damned fire-red hair of hers he was just itching to get his fingers into.

To prove it was only lack of shut-eye giving him such wild urges, he yawned.

How easy it would be to fall asleep.

To wake refreshed. Happy in the knowledge that Cass and her all-too-many temptations would soon be on their way.

Trouble was, he couldn't nap when he had work to do. Damned boring surveillance work that from this vantage point gave him a clear shot of a big chunk of the county along with all of Floyd's south pasture. It seemed unlikely that Zane would strike the same place twice, but he'd been dumb enough to do that very thing three times before, meaning at least odds were in Noah's favor. Once the kid had it in for someone, apparently he enjoyed terrorizing them again and again.

Rumor had it Floyd had ticked off not only Zane, but a bunch of other neighboring kids by blocking the dirt road cutting through his south pasture. If you happened to be a teen late for school, barreling down Floyd's rutted trail shaved a good twenty minutes off your trip.

Closing his eyes for a split second, Noah rubbed them with his thumb and forefinger. Hard to believe he'd once been as belligerent as any of the kids he was now constantly reprimanding. Just when he felt like rounding up the lot of them for a nice long stay at the county jail, Noah remembered himself at that age. And how old Sheriff Bowles had given him a second chance.

How would he have turned out if he hadn't been given that chance?

Hard to say.

Back then, with his folks always fighting, the only thing Noah had wanted was to escape. Fast cars, faster girls, fast-acting cheap booze that if only 'til the next morning's hangover somewhat dulled the pain. His parents had taught him early on that marriage was nothing more than one big fight. Yet what had he gone and done just as soon as he'd cleaned up his life? Hooked up with Darla.

One blustery long-ago October night, after drunkenly barreling his old Ford truck straight through Riverdale High's football field only to slam it head-on into the visitor's-side goalpost, Noah, his livid daddy, Sheriff Bowles and Coach Lockhart had all had a Come to Jesus meeting concerning the course Noah was taking with his life.

By the end of the hour lecture, over grim-faced handshakes, in exchange for not having Noah formally charged and sentenced, the men had agreed to tame him the old-fashioned way. Meaning Noah's father essentially turned his son over to the coach, who had in turn promised to make his life a living hell, starting off by ordering Noah to repair the damage he'd done to the field. From there, Noah was made slave to the team, always with the threat looming over his head that if he didn't do exactly as he was told, he'd be headed to the slammer instead of the locker room to pick up more dirty towels.

A year later, Noah ate, slept and breathed football—turned out he'd been pretty good at it, too.

A fact which he'd discovered by accident one day when he and quarterback Munchie Stevens had been out horsing around with the ball before practice. By the end of that week, Coach put Noah in the game as first-string running back. When Riverdale won that year's state championship and the next, scouts from all over had come to see him and his friends play.

It was no surprise when the University of Arkansas in Fayetteville offered Noah a full-ride scholarship.

His freshman year, he'd met up with Darla. She was a Tri-Delt. *Once you try Delta, you'll never go back.* Tall, blond, always telling him he'd hung her moon and her stars—damn he'd fallen quick.

Quick and hard.

Kind of the same way he'd died when after they'd gotten married the summer between his junior and senior years, that Dallas Cowboy agent had come sniffing around. Promising him things country boy Noah had never dared dream of. Cars, cash, houses, vacations…

That crisp autumn, he'd played like a well-oiled machine.

Flying like an angel, said the *Arkansas Democrat-Gazette.*

And then he'd dropped like a stone.

And all those dreams—*poof.*

Disappeared, just like all dreams tend to do when exposed to the sun. Just as magically as Darla had entered his life—she was gone. Presenting him with divorce papers just before Christmas break. Just after the team doctor had told him with a solemn shake of his head there was nothing more he could do.

Sorry son, but I'm afraid that knee's never gonna be right. We did all we could, but…

Swiping at a stupid sentimental tear for all that could have been, but was evidently never meant to be, Noah hardened his jaw and stared at that empty field, ignoring the dull ache in his knee.

Come first light, he had to get Cass and her brood not only out of his town, but out of his mind. Something about the way that woman looked at him—the way those precious babies looked at him—stirred old longings best left buried.

He'd tried the marriage route already. He'd sworn to love and protect and honor and cherish, and look what that'd gotten him. A big, fat divorce packet lying on his doorstep Christmas Eve.

Yep, he thought, gazing across Floyd's windswept fields dotted with round bales of hay and about four-dozen head of cattle. It was high time he swore off all women. Starting with Darla, adding every supposedly wounded member of that damned support group, and ending with Cass, every last one of them was trouble.

Trouble he'd lived half his life knowing full well to steer clear of.

So how come ever since Cass and her girls had entered his life, remembering his longtime vow to stay single was suddenly so—

A knock sounded at his patrol car's window.

Noah jumped a good six inches, sloshing hot coffee all over his bum knee. "Dammit!"

From outside came the low, familiar rumble of his dad's laughter. "Jimmy said I'd probably find you up here."

"Oh, he did, did he?" Noah scowled his way out of the car. After slamming the door, he flung what remained of his coffee into the weeds before setting the empty paper cup on the Blazer's hood. "Question is, what're you doing here?"

The older man took a deep breath, gazed up at the stars. "Just got in from the square dance up on Round Mountain. Checked my machine, and saw that for the fifth straight day you still hadn't called. What can I say? I was worried."

"Whoa," Noah said, narrowing his eyes. "Back up. You? Square dancing? What's up with that?"

"This dog might be old, but he ain't dead," his father said with a wink. "Speaking of which, heard you've been doing a little barking yourself. Wanna tell me about her?"

"No—and nice, subtle transition, there, Dad."

"I aim to please." Right hand pressed to his chest, he did a sure-footed jig, kicking up enough dust to choke a horse.

"You been drinking?" Noah asked.

"Just high on life, son. High on life. Now come on, tell me about her—or did you really think I came up here just to shoot the breeze with the likes of you?"

Chapter Seven

"You look awful," Cass said the next morning, watching Noah edge through the front door. His normally neat sandy brown hair stuck out at crazy angles, and Cass had to squelch the urge to smooth it back into place.

"Gee, thanks."

"I'm sorry," she said, "I didn't mean that in a bad way—more like I'm worried."

He shrugged.

Never a good sign where he was concerned.

"I made you breakfast," she said in front of the kitchen sink, glad she'd already dressed in another of her standard black dresses. Somehow, being dressed in her business armor—as her friend and co-worker, Chloe, dubbed Cass's seemingly endless array of black cotton, linen and silk—made her feel better equipped to deal with Noah. Not that being with him was a chore, but more like a lesson in frustration. Whenever she was even in the same room with him, she had a hard time knowing what to do with her hands. As for knowing what to say, she'd abandoned all hope of coming across as the confident, always composed businesswoman she was in Little Rock. For now, the best she could hope for was sounding logical!

"Great," he said, setting an official-looking beige hat on the counter. "I'm starved. What are we having? Eggs? Bacon?"

"Better," she said, drying her hands on a dishtowel before crossing to the stove. "An egg white, tofu and sprout omelet sprinkled with chives, fresh-squeezed orange juice and oat bran muffins with sugar-free plum preserves."

"Oh."

"Okay then," she said with forced cheer. "Let's eat. Today's a big day." While he took a seat at the cozy oak table, she bustled about the kitchen pouring their juice before taking the muffins from the oven. She put them in the cloth-draped basket she'd long since laid out on the counter, then added a pretty crystal bowl of preserves.

"Wow," he said once she'd joined him at the table. "This is quite a spread considering it's barely past seven. Thanks."

"You're welcome." When instead of eating, he just stared at his plate, she said, "Go on, dig in."

Looking almost reluctant, he finally reached for his fork.

After eating for a few minutes in companionable silence, and after wishing the fat-free meal filling her belly was having the same playful effect on them as their burger had yesterday at lunch, Cassie said, "I, um, rescheduled that Fayetteville limo service to take the babies and me home. They're going to put my car on a trailer.''

Over my dead and bloated body. Noah fisted the white cloth napkin she'd ironed, then slapped it to the table. ''Nope.''

''Excuse me?''

''Look,'' he said. ''I appreciate your having gone to the trouble of hiring a fancy limo service and all, but round here, we do things a little different.''

''Meaning?''

''Meaning, that a girl goes home with the man who brought her.''

''I'm still lost.''

He rubbed his hands over his eyes and sighed. ''I've already made plans to take you. I bought car seats. Jimmy's getting the department trailer out of storage.''

''But how is taking me back to Little Rock official business?''

''It just is, all right?'' Noah sighed.

It was official because getting her out of town was the only way he could figure to get his mind off her and her cute kids and back on his job. And since he'd been acting in a semiofficial capacity when he'd offered her roadside medical assistance, that made it his duty to see her safely home.

All the way home.

Even better, the trip would provide much-needed closure. Something about this curvy little health nut was a trifle too attractive, too tempting. Tempting for what, he wasn't sure. All he knew was that the sooner he got her out of his house, the better off he'd be.

"Noah, I'm perfectly capable of getting myself home, you know."

"Yes, I know," he said, "but I promised to take care of you the day we first met, and I damn well keep my promises."

Pushing her chair back from the table, Cass grabbed both of their plates and carried them to the sink. She'd finished her omelet, but Noah had hardly touched his. Just like he'd hardly touched her tofu alfredo the night before.

He had to start eating more of her healthy concoctions or her feelings were going to end up hurt. But then why did he even care? He'd already established the fact that she was going home—today.

"Look," he said. "This isn't a topic I generally talk about, but maybe you'll better understand where I'm coming from if I let you in on something."

She once again joined him at the table. "I'm listening."

He raked his fingers through his hair.

Stared out the window.

Sighed.

"Pretty early in my career," he said, "I was first on the scene of a wreck after a big ice storm. It was bad— the storm, but especially the wreck. After doing this work for a while, you can kind of bet sick odds on who's going to make it, and right off, I could tell the woman driver didn't have a chance."

Cassie covered her mouth with her hands.

"So anyway, I went ahead and called an ambulance. I mean, I'm all for miracles, but in the meantime, I felt so helpless. All I could do was sit there, holding her hand while she talked about her kids and husband, and how much she loved them. Elsie—that was her name—had two little boys. She wanted me to find their pictures in her purse, but seeing how there was now a tree where the passenger side used to be, I couldn't find it—her purse.'' Just thinking back to the horror of that day, Noah's pulse raced and his palms began to sweat.

"Her husband's name was Hank," he said a few minutes later. "Never forgot that. Toward the end, she said real plain, 'Tell Hank I love him. Tell him he was my best friend.'" Noah swiped at a few tears, sniffed. "So anyway, I felt responsible for her, Cass. I was in charge, and I let her die. On my watch, her life slipped right out of my hands."

Cassie shook her head. "That's crazy. She would've died whoever showed up first. And sounds to me like it was a good thing you were there. Who else would've made her last minutes count?"

"Doesn't matter," he said with a violent shake of his head. "I let her down, but that day on the side of the road with you, Cass, I told God He might've taken her, but He wasn't taking you—or your babies. I made a vow to watch out for you, and come hell or high water, that's exactly what I intend to do."

She stared at him, opened her mouth to say something, then clamped it shut, instead wrapping him in a hug.

"Noah…" A long time later, she pulled back, brushed the hair back from his forehead. "The fact that you feel compelled to see me and the girls all the way home is an incredibly heroic gesture, but completely unnecessary. I know you mean well, but the way you're so insistent on this point, it reminds me of the way Tom used to monitor my every move.''

''Yeah, but whereas your former schmuck of a husband was watching out for his monetary interests, I'm watching out for you.'' Standing, he said, ''Truth be told, I really haven't wanted you here, needing me 24/7, but helping you deliver Noelle and Hope was a pretty sacred moment for me, and no matter how awkward this is for us both, I'm afraid I have no choice but to watch out for you 'til you're all safely back in Little Rock.''

''But I already told you, I—''

Hands on her shoulders, he kissed her cheek. On the surface, it was an innocent kiss. One he would have given his favorite aunt Cookie. But the feelings that had been evoked by pressing his lips to Cassie's petal-soft cheek and breathing in her perfume were anything but friendly. They'd left him hungry. Wanting not her cheek pressed to his lips, but her mouth. He was tired of being her friend while wanting to be so much more. But why?

He made the mistake of looking at her.

Really looking at her.

At her jade-green eyes staring at him all wide-open and questioning, and he promised himself just as soon as he'd dropped her and her girls off at their home, he'd take a few days off. Go fishing. Maybe rent a cabin over in Eureka Springs and hang out counting squirrels. Anything, just so he'd never again have to see her pained look of bewilderment.

"Thanks again for breakfast," he finally said. "I'm going to grab a quick shower, then we'll be on our way."

JIMMY SLIPPED his key into the rusty padlock securing the gates to the Pritchett County storage lot, then pushed those gates open with a loud creak. After that, he swore he'd heard angels sing, for what else could be singing when he was gazing upon such a freakin' heavenly car?

There, before him, was all 186.3 inches of Cassandra Tremont's sleek yellow Thunderbird convertible.

And by God, given the choice between Pamela Anderson Lee agreeing to become his wife, or spending the rest of his life with this car, he'd have gone for the car.

And now, he was actually gonna get to drive her!

Sure, it might only be to load her onto the trailer, but that was enough. At least he could live out the rest of his life in peace knowing that they'd shared this one special time.

He pressed the keyless remote, happily sighing upon hearing her sweet chirp.

Easing his hand along the pale yellow finish, he curved his fingers under the door handle and eased it up, releasing the rich scents of full leather upholstery and spanking new carpet.

The dash was a little dusty, but he'd take care of that. After all, it was the least he could do. Now that

Cassandra had those other babies to deal with, she undoubtedly wouldn't be able to spend near enough quality time with this baby, but until turning her back over to her rightful owner, Jimmy'd see to it that she received proper care.

Settling onto the buttery-smooth leather seat, curling his fingers round the wheel, touching his feet to the pedals, Jimmy closed his eyes and swallowed hard.

The girl actually had him trembling, but that was okay.

She was hot.

A little excitement was to be expected on such a momentous occasion.

Slipping the key into the ignition, her 3.9L-4V V8 roared to life, and then he was easing the gearshift back, wishing she was a standard, but understanding that even rolling goddesses had their limitations.

His mission was to drive her right on up onto the trailer, but somehow that wasn't enough. Not near enough for a true fan such as himself.

He needed more time.

Time to tell her how much her page on that year's Ford calendar had meant to him. And how much he dearly longed to see how she'd handle out on the open road.

And then…before he'd even realized he'd done it, he was there.

Zooming down the open road at eighty-five.

Top down.

Winging around every curve as if the beauty rode on rails!

"Woo-hoo!" he called to the heavens.

Yes! Yes! This was just as he'd dreamed it would be and more. Sheer driving perfection in its purest form. Who cared that she was only to be his for this brief moment in time? This would have to be enough, for on his meager deputy's pay, he could never hope to buy her for his own.

Zoom!

He headed into the straight stretch just before Judi Thompson's place doing well over ninety.

Hot damn at the power!

He slowed her to sixty round the upcoming curve, then sadly to a measly fifteen for the s-curve after that.

And then—boom!

Just as he'd readied her for another straight stretch, he ran right into craft fair traffic.

Literally—ran right into!

Crash! The RV he'd hit might as well have been a brick wall.

Airbags inflated, Jimmy didn't feel all that hurt. As for his yellow baby, though…

Suddenly all of that dust on her dash didn't seem like her biggest problem.

"HERE YOU GO," Nurse Nosy said. "Just sign here and here, and these two sweeties are all yours."

They were all standing in the nursery after the girls had been fed and bathed and dressed in matching pink-and-purple gingham jumpers that Noah had given to her. Cassie thought them much cuter than the T-shirts she'd been given by the hospital.

"How about I just carry them out?" Noah asked, tickling twin tummies in their rolling bassinet.

"Sorry," the nurse said, "but it's hospital policy that all patients be wheeled out. That way, no one can say they didn't leave here in good condition."

"We at least get, like, a two-week warranty, don't we?" Noah asked with a wink. "After all, you get at least that with a new puppy or hamster."

Cassie poked him in his ribs. "For just once would you knock off the jokes? This is a solemn occasion."

"Darn straight," he said with a wink to the nurse over Cassie's head. "For the next eighteen years, you can kiss your freedom—not to mention, sleep—good-bye."

Rolling her eyes at him, Cassie signed the chart, then gazed upon her two miracles, but while the sight of their sheer perfection didn't surprise her, the look of wonder on Noah's face did. Each of his big, strong hands cocooned two baby feet, reminding her of his strength and goodness and warmth.

How different this day had been in her dreams. First, she'd planned to share it with Tom, then Chloe. But here, now, with Noah, a tingling in her heart told her everything was exactly the way it should be.

"Ready?" the nurse asked, shooting both of them a friendly smile.

Cassie nodded.

Noah jogged the few steps to the elevator to press the down button.

"Maybe I should take the stairs," he said when the

elevator didn't instantly appear. "That way I could have the truck all ready to go."

Hand on his forearm, Cassie said, "Noah, I already told you, we're taking a limo. You've already done so much. No way am I putting you to the trouble of driving us all the way to Little Rock."

"But the car seats."

"Thank you for those. It was very thoughtful. How much do I owe you?"

"Owe me?" The elevator dinged, and the nurse rolled the babies on while Noah placed his hand on the small of Cassie's back to guide her into the too-cramped space.

"You know, for the car seats?"

He hardened his jaw and his eyes narrowed to dangerous slits. "Thought we'd already been over this."

"We have. And I'm taking the limo." *Because if being this near you in an elevator makes my pulse race, I can't even imagine what sitting beside you for two hours is going to do!*

"No, Cass," he ground from between his teeth. "We haven't."

The elevator dinged, and the doors swished open.

Cassie drank gallons of fresh air.

The powdery sweetness of the babies combined with Noah's masculine scents would be her undoing. The leather of his worn deck shoes and faint citrus aftershave gave her an irrational craving to—

"Could y'all please settle this in the lounge area?" the nurse asked. "Other folks need to get on."

Cassie sharply looked away from Noah's handsome

profile to a small crowd of three well-dressed older women and a jumping girl of about five shrieking, "Grandma, look! I'm a frog! I'm a frog!" Each jump launched long black pigtails into flight.

"Samantha, pipe down," warned the tallest of the bunch. Grandma? A beautifully made-up grandma sporting hip jeans and an Abercrombie surf shirt!

"Noooaaah!" Samantha shrieked, hopping straight onto the elevator to crush her chubby arms around Noah's jean-clad legs. "I missed you! Where've you been? How come you left the wedding before the big party? There was cocktail weenies and cake and big shrimps! I wanted you to dance the Chicken Dance with me! You do that real good! Better than anyone!"

While Cassie backed off the elevator, the nurse and babies following, Noah swung the little girl into his arms for a warm hug. He smiled, but Cassie could've sworn that smile didn't quite reach his eyes. Who was this little cutie? And why did he look like holding her brought sadness rather than joy?

"Noah?" The woman Cassie presumed to be the girl's grandmother looked from Samantha to her to the babies. "Is this that gorgeous new family of yours I keep hearing so much about?"

Chapter Eight

Noah cringed.

As if this morning hadn't already gone straight down the toilet. The last person he needed to deal with was Kelsey's mom. And he'd been royally ticked at how just because he and Kelsey broke up, he never got to hang out with her family anymore—especially the munchkin currently in his arms.

This was just one more of his gripes with m-marriage—or any so-called relationship. They didn't last, and when they inevitably fell apart, all of those emotional ties fell apart right along with them.

And that hurt.

And he was tired of hurting.

"Yes, it's me, Evelyn," he said, exiting the elevator, Sammie still in his arms. She'd rested her head on his shoulder, and one of her chubby hands had hold of his right ear while the other landed on top of his head. He'd forgotten how nice it was holding kids. They always smelled great, too—like sweat and crayons and bubble gum. Every time Noah had broken things off with a woman, he'd lost another sweetie like Sam—

Kelsey's sister's kid. Tim—Tiffany's nephew. Lacey, Helen's niece. The list went on and on. Kids, just like the gorgeous women they'd been attached to, always left.

Yeah, but what if you had a kid of your own? Maybe even a perfect matching pair?

Noelle had gotten fussy, and Noah watched as Cassie scooped her out of the bassinet and into her arms.

"Ms. Tremont," the nurse said. "I'm really not allowed to let you—"

"Drop it," Noah barked. "Noelle's her baby and she can dam—darn well hold her if she pleases."

The nurse shot him a dirty look while Evelyn raised her eyebrows.

"On that note," Evelyn said, reaching for Sammie, "we'd better get upstairs. Rose Goodman just had another hip replacement surgery."

After easing Sammie into Evelyn's outstretched arms, Noah said, "Tell Rose I'll stop by after a while."

"Will do." Evelyn waved as she stepped onto the elevator behind the rest of her crew. Noah recognized the whole smiley bunch as being on the Cheer-Up committee from Riverdale Methodist Church. Funny though, how whenever he happened upon them they had this knack for making him grumpier than a fly on the wrong end of a swatter.

"Bye, Noah!" Sammie shouted as the elevator doors swished closed.

"She's adorable," Cass said as they resumed their walk to the hospital entrance. "And she seemed smitten with you. Another one of your many female fans, huh?''

When she winked before nudging him in his ribs, he frowned all the harder. ''Since I don't see any limos lurking about, guess I'll get the truck.''

''I told them noon and it's just now eleven-thirty-five. Who'd have thought we'd be running ahead of schedule?'' She shot him a grin.

''Look, Cass, I—''

''Sheriff!'' Out of breath, cheeks blaze red and uniform all rumpled and sweaty, Briggs chugged through the hospital's automated main entry. ''Thank God I found you! We've been callin' and pagin' you for like an hour!''

Noah automatically reached for his phone, but it wasn't in its usual spot on the waistband of his jeans. Neither was his pager. Oops. Big oops. It wasn't like him to be so forgetful. But then it also wasn't like him to be so wound up over a woman and her babies! ''Well? What's up?''

''It's Jimmy. Ambulance is bringin' him in with a busted arm. And ma'am,'' he said, removing his hat to hold it over his heart. ''I'm real sorry to have to tell you this, but you've got yourself a seriously busted car.''

CASSIE SQUEEZED Noelle a bit tighter.

Seeing Jimmy, all pale and broken and bruised, had been bad enough. But standing outside the hospital's emergency room in blinding noonday sun, watching her poor car being towed through the lot, left her feeling faint. The tow guy was a friend of Jimmy's, apparently, and had stopped by to check on him.

Leaning hard against Noah, she said, "Ouch."

"That's one way of putting it." He held Hope, and somehow, being close like this, the four of them together, made the sight of her crunched, not even one-year-old yellow baby somewhat easier to bear.

"What am I going to do?" she asked.

Behind her, she felt Noah shrug. "Guess there's only one thing to do. We head on to Little Rock, and I'll get Moe down at The Dent Doctor to give her a look."

"Does he have the expertise to work on this car?"

Laughing, Noah said, "Our illustrious ex-mayor drives a Lamborghini he's always dinging, and Precious Hallowell has a brand spankin' new Porsche she just backed into her garage—her closed garage. So, yeah, I'd say he knows what he's doing."

"O-okay."

A flash of sun glinted off the trunk of a black Caddie pulling into the lot. Cassie groaned.

"What's wrong now?"

"The limo. I forgot all about the limo." Glancing at her watch, she saw that the whole mess with Jimmy and her car had taken well over an hour, which meant the limo service she'd ordered all the way from Fayetteville would now be long gone. "Grrr. Why didn't someone find me? I could have said quick goodbyes to Jimmy and my car, then been on my way."

His free hand on her shoulder, Noah turned her to face him. "Relax. This at least settles the debate over who's driving you." Grinning, he said, "Looks like I win. So if you're ready, let's go."

Gazing up at him, at his deep brown eyes, she shook her head. "I don't think so."

"What's that mean? You wanna stop off at Brenda's for one last burger before we go?"

She shook her head.

"Then what?"

"I'm not going. I, um, think it'd be best if I stayed here until my car is fixed. This Moe person is going to need all kinds of insurance information, and there's going to be paperwork and stuff." *And something about the way you have one hand on my baby, and the other on me, I just don't feel strong enough to deal with a crunched car and two newborns and a big house and my business just yet. Maybe tomorrow. But not today.*

"Um, all right." Releasing her, he took a step back. "Um, yeah, sure. I guess that works."

"If you don't want us at your house, I understand. As soon as the craft fair's over, I'm sure we can find—"

Not want you?

Noah swallowed hard. That was the problem. He did want her. And her babies. And her disgustingly healthy cooking and too much cleaning and her laugh and wide, green eyes that drew him in like warm, clear Beaver Lake water on a hot summer's day.

Across the parking lot, those three gigglers he'd seen at Brenda's hustled into the hospital dressed in cute candy striper uniforms. Noah took Cass's hand in his and said, "Nope, you're all coming home with me—for however long it takes to fix your car."

"But, Noah, I—" Since he had no free hands, meaning he couldn't silence her by pressing his fingers to her lips, he went with his only other option, which meant covering her mouth with his own.

Noah's kiss eased through Cassie's body like calm in a bottle. Maybe it was the sunshine raining down on them, or the powdery-sweet smell of her babies nestled between them or the even sweeter smell of spring making her arms and legs all quivery, but whatever the cause, she knew she never wanted the delicious sensation to end.

Then it did, and it took her a second to find the strength to open her eyes.

"Sorry," Noah said, releasing her hand before taking a couple steps back.

"Sure," Cassie said. *And if I act bored enough, maybe you'll believe that kiss affected me as little as it evidently did you.*

"Must've been the heat," he said, lips pressed to the top of Hope's down-covered head.

Turning away from the enchanting sight of her beautiful baby and the breathtakingly handsome man holding her, Cassie studied a trio of sparrows splashing in a puddle left from the hospital's automatic sprinklers. The perimeter of lawn looked so perfect it could've been colored with Crayola green. "Of course."

"Speaking of which, we'd better get these munchkins out of the sun. Don't want them burned."

"No. That wouldn't be good." Geesh, was she like

the worst new mother in the world? Following Noah to his truck, Cassie wanted to have been the one concerned about the babies getting sunburned—not Noah! Not the cold, unfeeling creep who'd kissed her like she'd never been kissed before only to now act like it'd meant nothing!

Two rows over, a truck belched by, tainting the air with caustic exhaust.

"Cover Hope's nose!" she cried.

"Why?" He walked backward for the second it'd taken to ask the question.

"Because exhaust fumes are toxic! And stop walking backward. You could trip."

"And you're worried about me getting hurt?"

"Not you—Hope!"

Stopping beside his faded red Suburban, he said, "You're ticked at me, aren't you?"

"No."

"Liar." He playfully tugged a chunk of her hair.

"Ouch."

"Oh, that didn't hurt, and you know it."

"Did so," she said, studying the Juicy Fruit wrapper some litterbug had left at her feet. She knelt to grab the gum wrapper. Her girls deserved a nice, tidy earth.

"Tell me the truth." Noah said, slipping his hand about her waist when she'd stood back up. "You're mad because I thought about the babies getting sunburned before you."

"You couldn't be more wrong."

"Then how come your lips are doing that sexy frowny thing they do when you think I haven't eaten enough of whatever healthy tofu/bug combo you've served me?''

"I've never served you bugs, and as for my lips, they—'' Cheeks hot, she touched those lips with her fingers, swearing they were still tingling from his kiss.

He thought they were sexy, huh? Her lips?

The mere thought only made them tingle more!

"I'm sorry,'' he said, releasing her to fish his keys from his pocket. "That came out wrong.''

Walking around to the passenger side of his truck, he opened the back door and settled Hope into her baby seat. Once he'd clicked her safety harness into place, he reached for Noelle, then opened Cassie's door. "Climb in. I'll make sure Munchkin Number Two's locked and loaded.''

Though Cassie wanted to glare at him for using such rough and ready guy slang in reference to her perfectly pink little girl, when she gazed into his gorgeous, deep brown eyes, then lowered her gaze to where Noelle rested her cheek on his broad chest, all she could do was smile.

"OKAY,'' NOAH SAID from his perch on the sun-flooded window seat in Cass's room. "This time, pay attention. You take the sticky thingy and put it here—not on the ducks.''

"But it looks cuter on the ducks.''

"Cass…'' Noah sighed. "This isn't about cute. It's about keeping the wet stuff in the diaper and not on our laps.''

"I see your point.'' Practicing what he'd just taught

her using Hope as his demo baby, Cass expertly changed Noelle's diaper. "There, how's that?" she asked, proudly holding her squirming baby up for his inspection.

"Much better. In a few hours, we'll move on to baths." After getting Hope back into her clothes, having a devil of a time working her tiny buttons and snaps, he ambled into the kitchen, looking for a snack.

Unfortunately, Cass was right on his heels as he reached into the cabinet beside the fridge for one of his favorite chocolate fudge snack cakes. "Gone," she said, smug smile playing about her lips.

"What do you mean, gone?"

"I mean, those things aren't healthy. Too much hydrogenated stuff and monotriglycerides."

"What're those?"

"I'm not sure," she said, reaching into the fridge. "But here, have this."

She handed him an apple.

Oh boy.

"Look," he said, trying his damnedest to not be distracted by the warm and fuzzies shooting through his chest from Hope snoozing on him. Oblivious to her mother's wicked ways, she'd rested her head on his shoulder, and her five pound body felt like a warm bean bag in his arms. A bean bag with a heart beating against his chest. Fast beats. But that was okay. Baby hearts did that.

He remembered from holding his ex-girlfriend Diane's niece, Heather—who was now eight and trying out for pee-wee cheerleader. Where did the time go?

Where did the children go? And why was it he still didn't have a kid—or a baker's dozen of 'em—to call his own?

Gee, could it be because you can't commit?

Scowling, he moved on to his next favorite cabinet. The one over the dishwasher where he kept chips.

He'd just touched his hand to the door handle when Little Miss Food Police said, "Nope. I saved you from those, too. Too much salt. Salt's our enemy."

"Look." His hand cupping Hope's head, Noah sighed before turning to face her mother. "We need to talk."

"About better nutrition?"

He forced a grin. "Maybe another time."

"Then what?"

"Ever heard that old saying about a man's house being his castle?"

"Sure, but I prefer to insert woman for man."

He rolled his eyes.

"Come on Noelle," he said, taking her from Cass. "We're going on a date."

"You can't just take them," she said, following him and both of her babies into the living room where with no hands he managed just fine to slip on deck shoes, grab his wallet and keys, then nudge open the screen door.

"Sorry," he said. "May I please take the girls on a brief date?"

"Yes, you may. But what about me?"

"Do you plan on talking nutrition?"

"If you want."

"Yeah, well I *don't* want."

She dropped her green gaze. "O-okay."

Man, how did she do this?

The woman had just thrown out at least fifty bucks worth of awesome junk food, yet with one glance—or rather lack of a glance—he was the one feeling like he'd done something wrong!

Standing outside the screen door, still holding the munchkins, he said, "Ms. Tremont, if it so pleases you, would you accompany us to Brenda's where I plan on giving your most lovely daughters a valuable lesson on true nutrition?"

After giving him what he now recognized as her most scathing look, she begrudgingly opened the door.

Chapter Nine

"Wow," Cassie said, catching the cascading sheet of chocolate from her dip cone before it landed on her clean shirt. "This is good—I've never had one before—but hazardous."

"Tell me about it," he said, licking the edge of his cone to catch stray drips. He eyed the babies who were sound asleep in their carriers. "I thought they'd like a cone, too, but I guess this mission was a little premature."

"You think?" She shot him a grin.

"Well, hey, at least one good thing came out it."

"What's that?"

"I got you to try another form of junk food, and from the looks of it, you're enjoying it."

"Am not," she said though an extra-large, wafer-thin section of chocolate.

Noah swallowed hard even though he currently didn't have a drop of ice cream in his mouth.

Cass had closed her eyes on her lick around the cone. In the process driving him wild with her darting pink tongue. He squeezed his eyes shut. What the woman did to him with just one of those innocent smiles should be criminal.

"Noah?"

"Huh?"

"You okay?"

"Ah, sure, why wouldn't I be?"

"I don't know, but while you've been staring at me, your ice cream just dripped down your sleeve."

"Aw, hell," he said, eyeing the goopy spill. Snatching a wad of napkins from the dispenser on the table, he said, "Guess my mind was a million miles away."

"Thinking 'bout work?"

I wish! "Nah… Just stuff."

"What kind of stuff?"

Oh, things like how much I'd like to try kissing you again, but how you being a new mommy and all, makes you off limits. And how I have no right to even be thinking such impure thoughts, but that lately, I can't seem to help it.

He shrugged. "You know. Stuff."

"Sure." She licked again.

"What?" he asked when she still hadn't wiped that stricken look from her face.

"I miss you, that's all."

"What do you mean? I'm right here."

Finishing off her cone, she shook her head. "You haven't been with me since the first time we kissed."

"What's that supposed to mean?"

"You tell me."

"Aw, geez." He looked across the room to see Zane up to his usual no good. Using a pocketknife, he was painstakingly carving something into Brenda's varnished oak tabletop. Around these parts, a right of passage. Shoot, Noah had his own name linked with Vicki Hayes's inside the confines of a crudely carved heart over on table fifteen. But seeing how Zane was already carrying a full load of trouble, and his fingertips were still stained neon green from the spray paint that'd been used to give the bronze statue of Riverdale's first mayor a new toupee, and seeing how Cass's invasive stare had long since put him on edge, he said, "Hang tight. Duty calls."

"What's wrong?" she asked, following his gaze.

"See that kid?"

"Yeah."

"He's trouble."

Just as Noah slid out of the booth, Zane looked up, knife still in hand.

Easing past the chairs of the few thankfully oblivious afternoon diners, Noah slid onto the booth seat across from Zane, and before the boy knew what hit him, he took the knife from his hand, folded it, then raised up to slip it into his right front pocket.

"Hey!" Zane protested. "You can't do that."

"Just did."

"Yeah, well, my daddy's gonna come down here and kick your—"

"Tough words considering right about now your daddy's prob'ly downing his sixth beer of the day."

"Go to hell," the boy snarled. "And while you're at it, mind your own damned business."

"Be glad to, only at the moment, you carvin' up Brenda's table is kinda my business."

Zane rolled his dark eyes. "Everybody knows you done the same and worse."

"That make it right?"

He shrugged.

Noah leaned closer. "Tell you something else I'll bet you don't know. Unlike you, Brenda caught me carving up her table. I had to wash dishes for her after school for two months or Sheriff Bowles promised to lock me up."

"Shows just how dumb you were." Unscrewing the lid on the salt shaker, Zane put a napkin over it, then flipped it upside down before sliding the napkin out. "Hell, I'd have to steal a car to end up in a juvie home—maybe even knock off a bank. And there's nobody round here smart enough to make charges stick."

Noah closed his eyes and sighed. "You are one tough cookie."

"Damned straight."

"It ever occur to you that seeing how I used to be just like you, I know you?"

"Here we go." Now the kid was rolling his eyes. "This the part of your speech where you turn all shrink on me? Zap me with reverse psychology?"

"Wouldn't dream of it."

Brenda delivered Zane's order of fries and a Coke. "Everything all right here?" she asked, eyeing Noah.

"Peachy," Noah said, snatching a wad of the kid's fries.

"Hey!"

"Like being robbed, do ya?"

"You see that?" he asked Brenda.

"See what?" she asked, already on her way back to the kitchen.

"This is police harassment," the kid said. "My daddy's gonna be on you like fly on—"

"Watch it," Noah said, voice lethally low. "There are ladies and children present."

"Like I give a rat's—"

"Stop. Stop the whole tough guy routine. Stop acting like you don't care that your dad's a drunk and your mother killed herself the night you made your first soccer goal."

"Shut up."

"Stop acting like it doesn't matter your girl, Heidi, is dating Eric Denton, even though she went with you all through ninth grade."

"Screw you. You don't know sh—"

Noah slapped his palms on the table, rattling the ice in Zane's Coke. "What I know is that it's high time you grew up. Yeah, life's dealt you some pretty crappy blows, but then I can't count on one hand the number of folks round here leadin' fairy-tale lives."

"Boo, freakin', hoo." Gaze bored and glassy, Zane leisurely chewed a fry.

BACK AT Noah's house, while Cassie was still unfastening Hope's car seat, Noah already held Noelle in his arms, and was almost to the front door. By the time Cassie caught up to him, he was in the sun-flooded kitchen, staring at the open fridge. "What're you looking for?'' she asked, cradling Hope close. ''Maybe I can help.''

''Doubt it,'' he said, slamming the door.

''Ready to talk about it?''

'''Bout what?''

''Whatever's been eating you since we left Brenda's. Does it have something to do with that kid?''

He turned away from her, but she put her hand on his shoulder, urging him back. ''Please don't shut me out,'' she said. ''For better or worse, we're roomies. If I can, I'd like to help.''

''Forget it. The kid's unredeemable.''

''He's that far gone?''

''Yep.'' Toying with one of Noelle's red curls, he said, ''I might feel different if I had my own kid. I might know what to do. Where to start. As is, I—'' He shrugged. ''I've gotta catch a few winks before work. You all right?''

''Sure.'' *It's you I'm worried about.*

''Cool.'' In the living room, he eased a sleeping Noelle into her portable carrier and fastened her safety harness.

''No,'' Cassie said, doing the same with Hope. ''Now that I've had a second to think about it, it's not *cool*. And we never did finish our conversation from back at Brenda's.''

''I'm bone tired,'' he said with a put-upon sigh. ''Can't all of this wait until later?''

''No. Right now, tell me why you're so standoffish. Tell me what it is about that kid that's got you so tense that little muscle keeps popping in your jaw.'' She touched it. ''There. Just then. Did you feel that?''

Reaching up, Noah covered her fingers with his own, pressing them into his cheek. *What I feel is you touching me, emotions I'm not equipped to handle bearing down on me.*

''That popping is a sign,'' she said. ''Means you're too tense. You need a release.'' She slipped her fingers out from under his, then stepped behind him, easing her thumbs into his aching shoulders and neck. ''See? You're a brick wall.''

Eyes closed, Noah surrendered to the liquid warmth her nimble fingers poured through him. In his mind, he saw her full lips wrapping round the N in his name. Imagined the feel of her breasts mounding against his chest. And it was then he found the real meaning of the word release by easing around to take Cass into his arms. Lift her effortlessly off of her feet with one arm around her hips, the other under the heavy fall of her hair, pressing his lips to hers.

''Mmm...'' she groaned.

Yes, he silently said. *Give me release. Release me from my job frustrations. From all of the things in my life I've always wanted changed, but have been powerless to do a damned thing about. From the loneliness that until meeting you, I hadn't even realized had been so bad.*

She mewed beneath him, and he deepened the kiss still, parting her lips with his tongue, tasting the hint of vanilla ice cream still lingering on the damp pillow of her breath.

This was insanity.

This kissing her, this wanting her, yet he physically could not stop.

"Noah," she said, driving him further over the edge just whispering his name.

On a ragged groan, he returned his angel to her feet. "I'm sorry," he said. "I didn't mean to do that. Would never ordinarily do that. But I'm tired, and…"

Her slight, quivering hand again cupping his cheek, she said, "What if I wanted you to do that?"

"Then you'd be wrong."

"Shouldn't I be the judge of that?"

"No." Hell, no.

Because I know I'm right. You deserve a good man. A family man who doesn't have my hang-ups over the institution of marriage. And there, for the first time in his adult life, he'd actually thought the word without stuttering, meaning his convictions to steer clear of her—and all women—had to be right.

"No? Would you listen to yourself? You might be the law around this town, Noah Wheeler, but that doesn't give you jurisdiction over my heart."

Heading to his room for a cold shower, he said, "It was just a kiss, Cass. It had nothing to do with your heart."

Cassie started to follow him, but stopped herself at the start of the hall.

He was right.

She knew the perils involved with opening her heart. Just like she knew it was high time she give up on this fantasy world of Noah being her protector, and once and for all see this picture for the way it really was.

All they shared other than that one insanely intimate moment on the side of a lonesome highway was a roof over their heads.

In a few days, her car would be fixed and she'd be safely back in Little Rock, never to see him again.

"HE STRUCK AGAIN, Sheriff, and this time I want justice." Floyd stood with his legs spread, hands fisted on his hips beside a smoldering pile of debris that had once been one of his best outbuildings. A pile of beer cans and broken wine bottles further attested to Zane's wild night. The whole mess stank beneath the glare of hot morning sun—and Noah wasn't just talking about the souring booze.

He rubbed his aching neck.

"You hear me, and hear me well," Floyd said, spindly index finger poking Noah's chest. "That boy's a menace who's got to be stopped. While you been over to your house playin' nursemaid to that gaggle of gals, I've been—"

"Don't touch me," Noah growled. "And as for what I do in my free time, that's my business."

"Unless it takes your mind off the thugs terrorizing innocent hardworking folks. Where were you last night when you were supposed to be looking over my place?"

Noah clenched his teeth.

Where had he been? Sleeping. In all the hubbub over getting the twins settled—not to mention trying to forget the havoc their momma was wreaking upon his heart, Noah had forgotten to set his alarm.

"You lock that boy up tight, Sheriff. Lock him up, or as long as there's breath in my body, I'll see to it you never win another election."

BONE TIRED, Noah pulled into his driveway later that morning planning on heading straight back to bed. He creaked open the door of his SUV, eased his feet out and stood, slamming the door shut. The noise echoed through the still-quiet neighborhood where the only sounds besides a few chirping swallows were the shouts of the Jenson kids playing down the street and the swish of Obert Undem's sprinkler.

He yawned, easing his face back to catch the sun, and when he was again looking straight, he saw her.

Cass.

Sitting sideways on his porch swing, painting her toenails. Looking prettier than any woman had the right to in another of her seemingly endless supply of black sundresses. The garment had risen up, and if he'd allowed his gaze to stray where it truly wanted to go, he'd have spied the barest hint of black panties hugging the sweet curve of her behind. She wore her hair in a neat ponytail, and his mind strayed again, wondering what she'd look like with that red silk she called hair all messy and buck wild.

"Hey," she said, her sleepy smile warming him a thousand times more than the sun.

"Hey, yourself. Those babies of yours let you rest?"

"A little," she said, covering a small yawn. She laughed. "Okay, maybe very little."

"You look pretty," he said because he was tired and couldn't stop himself. Lazy rays of sun glinted fire off of the red in her hair. "And I like those hot pink toes." *And I'd like 'em even better had I painted them myself while you lounged all satisfied and lazy in the tub after we've just made love.*

"Thanks," she said, giving them a saucy wriggle. "I'm trying to steal a little time for myself in between all those diaper changes." She strained to reach the last few toes on her left foot.

"I'm glad," he said, taking the polish and brush thingee from her. "Here, let me help."

"Sure. Thanks."

The toes he painted didn't turn out quite as perfect as hers, but they didn't look all bad even if he did say so himself.

"Hungry?" she asked, patting the empty portion of the seat beside her as he screwed the lid on the polish, then handed it to her.

"Nah." He eased onto the swing. "I grabbed a breakfast burrito at Brenda's."

"Mmm, sounds healthy." She winked.

Grinning, he shrugged.

From behind the screen door, one of the babies cried. "Oops," she said, putting her palm on his bum knee for leverage as she hobbled off of the swing. "Duty calls."

"That would be Noelle," he said, following her into

the house with a wince. "And from the sounds of it, she needs a new diaper."

"And you know this how?" she asked on their way down the hall.

"I'm their daddy. I should know."

Even though there'd been a humorous note in his tone, Cassie bit her tongue to keep from snapping her usual retort. Once they reached the babies, and Noah saw for himself that he didn't know everything there was to know about the pink duo, he'd be properly reminded that he was no more their daddy than he was the state's governor!

But then she entered the bedroom, setting her polish on the dresser before kneeling beside the blanket-lined drawer doubling as a crib. Noah had been right on one count—it was Noelle crying.

Okay, so Cassie gave him bonus points for knowing Noelle's voice, but as for that diaper bit, that was nuts. She was Noelle's mother, and couldn't yet tell which of her cries meant what.

More to make Noah feel important than because she thought her daughter had already wet the diaper she'd changed only thirty minutes earlier, Cassie gave the smooth plastic mound a pat. "There. It's—" It'd been on the tip of her tongue to say bone dry, but just as he'd predicted, it was fat. Meaning in diaper terminology—wet.

Rising, hugging her baby to her shoulder, Cassie asked, "How did you know?"

"I already told you," he said with a rogue's wink. "I know these things. I'm her daddy."

At that moment, gazing upon Noah's handsome features backlit by morning sun, gazing upon her baby as if she was the most beautiful sight he'd ever seen, oh, how Cassie wished he truly were Noelle's father. Selfishly not for her daughter—but herself.

"MM-MMM," Noah's dad said Thursday night over a heaping plate of tofu and eggplant lasagna. "This sure does hit the spot."

"It hits something," Noah mumbled under his breath.

"What was that, Son?"

His dad and Cass eyeing him, Noah forced down his latest bite of dinner with a good, long swig of iced herbal tea, then forced a smile. "Nothing."

Not a doggone thing, if he steered clear of the fact that Cass hadn't had any business inviting his old man over for dinner in the first place—apparently they'd gotten to know each other during one of his dad's daily calls. Not to mention the fact that Noah didn't exactly feel comfortable with his past and present being seated at the same table. The very same table where Noah had grown up learning by his father's own example that marriage wasn't for him!

"So, Cass," his dad said, annoying Noah further by calling Cassie by the nickname *he'd* coined. "Tell me why you're in such an all-fire hurry to get back to Little Rock, when my boy here could do with a lot more of this home cooking."

Noah's stomach clenched when she flashed his old

man a big beautiful smile. "Aren't you a charmer," she said. "Just like your son."

While his dad beamed, taking yet another bite of the noxious meal, Noah stared at his plate, squeezing his fork tightly.

"Yep, the women in that so-called support group of his—"

"It's not mine."

His dad eyed him a good long while before clearing his throat. "As I was saying, the women round this town sure have given my boy a hard time. The way I see it, you, Ms. Cassie Tremont, are a much needed breath of fresh air."

"Well, thank you," she said with a pretty blush. "That's the nicest thing anyone's said to me in a while."

Oh, that did it!

Noah knew darned well just the other day he'd told her she looked pretty. At least he thought he had. Maybe. Well, if he hadn't, he was going to. Then she'd be flashing him that toothy grin instead of his dad!

Whoa, there big fella. Weren't you the man who just swore off all women—most especially Cass?

"Noah?" Cass said, her fingers curved round his forearm, setting off all manner of internal sparks. "Are you okay? You seem awfully quiet."

"Probably he's thinkin' about work," his dad said. "Got one heckuva nasty case brewin'."

"Oh?" Cass asked, eyebrows raised as if inviting his dad to expound.

Noah put his napkin on the table and pushed back

his chair. "Speaking of work, let me wash up these dishes, then I'm outta here."

"So soon?" Cass said. "But I made fat-free blueberry cobbler for dessert."

"You go on, son. I'll eat your share."

"Gee, thanks," Noah said, clinking his plate into the sink.

"You just go on about your business," his dad said. "Let me worry about cleaning up."

"Boy," Cass said with an easy grin. "A girl could get used to having two handsome fellas fight over who's going to do dishes."

Noah snatched his hat off of the counter, then said in low tones to Cass, "Come here." Taking her by her elbow, he led her out of her chair and to the front door, a spot he hoped was well out of earshot of his prying old man.

"What's wrong?" she asked when he opened the front door and edged her outside—just in case.

"What's wrong?" He laughed. "My father is flirting with you. That's what's wrong."

"Oh, he is not," she said, swatting his chest. He trapped her hand there against his thundering heart by putting his own hand on top of it. Her fingers were long and thin, elegant and soft. In contrast, his were big and rough and gawky. He had no business wanting this woman.

Even so, he hardened his jaw and said, "He *is* flirting with you, and I don't like it."

"Why, Sheriff Wheeler, you wouldn't be jealous, would you?"

"No. Hell, no. Just make sure he's out of here at a decent hour."

"Yes, sir. Am I allowed to watch TV and talk on the phone after he leaves, or should I go straight to bed?" Even with only the dim streetlight illuminating her porcelain-fine features, he caught that sassy twinkle in her eyes.

"Go straight to bed," he growled, slipping his free hand about her waist before cinching her close.

"And then what?" she asked, her hot breath fanning his lips.

Think of me. Dream of me. Imagine my hands skimming over your belly and breasts.

Since he couldn't say such outrageous things, he kissed the words into her.

He kissed her hard, soft, hungry, and when he'd had his fill of reminding her who was the man of the house, he softened his touch, easing his fingers up under the spill of her long, soft hair, brushing her tongue with his, reveling in the guttural mews urging him on from somewhere deep in her throat.

When he released her, she looked good and dazed.

He hated himself for liking it.

"Wow," she finally said. "That's, um, an awful lot to remember."

"Yeah, well…" He kissed her again. On the tip of her nose. "Just see that you do."

He winked before walking into the night.

IT WAS TEN before Noah's dad left, and a minute past ten before Cassie made it to the kitchen phone to punch in what was sadly becoming a familiar number.

After two rings, an equally familiar voice said, "Brenda's Bigger Burger—Brenda speaking."

"Um, hi," Cassie said, swinging the long phone cord like a jump rope on the kitchen floor. "Um, are you still open for deliveries?"

A snort came through loud and clear over the line. "Now, why would I be answerin' if I wasn't still open? This you, Red? Cravin' another double cheeseburger?"

"I, um, think I must be low on iron."

"Among other things."

Cassie chose to ignore Brenda's latest taunt.

The things she'd learned to put up with for a little grease!

This time of night, Cass would've settled for more of Noah's front porch kissing, but seeing how the big, kissing creep had just sauntered off—even whistling as he'd sauntered—well, was it any wonder she'd now been reduced to your common, everyday variety grease-a-holic?

"Want Tator Tots with your burger?"

"Yes, please."

"Chocolate malt?"

"If it's not too much trouble."

Brenda graced her with another snort.

"Yancie already went home for the night, but me and Ernie'll drop this stuff off on our way home."

"Thank you, Brenda."

"You're welcome, *Red.*"

Chapter Ten

"Wait," Noah said Saturday afternoon on his backyard deck, reigning supreme over his grill in khaki shorts and a faded blue Bad Bubba's Bar-B-Que T-shirt. The sweet smell of the barbecued chicken he was tormenting Cassie with made her mouth water. Would he ever pronounce it done? "Let me guess? In addition to double cheeseburgers and chocolate dip cones, you've never had barbecue, either?"

Smiling at the butterfly that had landed on sleeping Hope's tummy, she said, "Yes, I have had barbecue, thank you very much. But it's always been served away from the grill. Smelling it up close like this, it's—"

"Really got your juices flowing?" He winked.

"No. I'm just hungry. And what's with that naughty winking? Got something stuck in your eye?"

Just the sight of finger-lickin' good you. Empowered by that manly streak that always accompanied an afternoon spent grilling, Noah planted a quick kiss to her cheek, losing himself not in the scent of barbecue sauce but the fragrance of her perfume.

Two backyards down, Obert Undem yanked his ancient mower to life, bringing Noah back to reality.

"Sorry," he mumbled, no longer Grill Man, Master of his Universe, but just a guy, wanting to kiss a girl he had no business kissing.

Furious over forgetting this fact yet again, Noah turned his back on Cass's sexy pout, bracing his forearms on the deck rail while staring across the yard.

The mower engine sputtered and died.

Obert sputtered a string of curses.

Somewhere in the dappled shade, a squirrel chattered.

Birds chirped and a light breeze rustled leaves.

Cassie looked away from Noah's strong back, preferring instead to remember his oh-so-handsome face that held the power to weaken her knees and befuddle her senses. Why did he always do that? Kiss her then apologize? Or like that night on the porch, kiss her then walk away?

Even worse, why did she care? Okay, yes, so he'd safely delivered her babies. Yes, they'd shared his house for a few days, but beyond that what did they have in common?

Watching him brush a nonexistent dust speck from Hope's cheek, then scoot her carrier deeper into the shade of a towering oak, Cassie further acquiesced that okay, he did seem to feel a certain affection for her girls. So at least they had that in common, but beyond that—nada.

He hated her every choice in food. And she hated—okay, so maybe hate was a bit strong for the way she'd felt about that juicy double cheeseburger, or the delectable chocolate dip cone, but still, for the most part, their food choices weren't even remotely compatible.

And look at their houses. Hers was a stark study in sleek modern lines. Plenty of chrome and stainless steel and bold reds and blues splashed upon soaring walls. Aside from her room, his house was the kind of homespun accidental hodgepodge that couldn't be designed, but like cave formations, had to grow slowly over time.

For that matter, they probably wouldn't even enjoy the same vacation spots. He was probably the theme park type while for her last vacation, she and Tom had lounged in the lap of luxury in Tahiti.

Squeezing her eyes briefly shut on the amazing time they'd shared, along with the fact that at least on Tom's part, every second they'd ever spent together had been a lie, she forced herself to ask, "If you could go anyplace in the world right now, where would it be?"

"Moot question, seeing how I obviously can't."

"Oh, come on," she said, giving his forearm a squeeze. "Humor me, and play along."

He sighed. "It's stupid, seeing how I'll never in a million years on my salary afford to go."

"So what if it is stupid? Tell me anyway. And who knows?" she teased, brandishing her own naughty wink. "Maybe one of these days you'll win the lottery. Or go above and beyond your standard serve and protect, and somebody you save might give you a handsome reward."

"Nah, in the first place, we don't get too many rich folks in need of rescue round here—well, save for you."

Funny how, yes, she had plenty of paper money, but lately, even if she'd had all the money in the world, emotionally she'd still be dirt poor. "There are other kinds of riches, you know."

"Try telling that to my truck," he said with a snort. "It's needed a new transmission for going on two years."

"I'm being serious."

"I know," he said, leaving the grill to cup her cheeks with his big, sun-warmed hands. The sight of him stole her breath. Searching brown eyes, luminous and warm, framed by laugh lines in their corners. Whisker-stubbled cheeks ruddy and tanned. At that moment, just seeing his face overrode all else. Her babies. Her job. Everything. Distilling her life to but one shining goal—being gifted with another of his salty-sweet kisses. So much so did she yearn to press her lips to his, that they'd taken on an aching hum. "Tahiti."

"What?" she squeaked. Hadn't they been talking kisses?

"You asked where I most wanted to go. Tahiti."

Cassie swallowed hard. If only she could go again. Experience it anew through Noah's eyes, through his touch, through sweet summer storms of his kisses. Then she'd be free of Tom's lies. She'd start her life anew.

Why wouldn't Noah open himself to her? Why did

he keep drawing her in only to push her away? Why did her chest ache with wondering? Why couldn't she focus on the fact that in just a few more days she'd be away from him? Away from the all-American, all-too-inviting scents of his barbecue and fresh-mown back-yard with it's chattering squirrels and butterflies and most important—him?

"T-that sounds nice," she said. "I've heard it's really lovely."

"Stop," he said.

"Stop what?"

"Pretending for my sake you've never been."

"I wouldn't do that."

"Bull. Because you just did. I'm a big boy, Cass. I know our worlds are a million miles apart."

"Is that why you apologize whenever you kiss me?"

He shrugged, turned the chicken on the grill before brushing on more sauce.

"Please answer me," she said, fingers curved around his bicep, wondering what those arms of his would feel like were she to wrap her fingers round them naked....

"I apologize for one simple reason," he said.

"And that would be?"

"Because it's wrong. Kissing you. Holding you." He swallowed. "All wrong."

"Why?"

"Because it'll never go beyond that." Looking away from her, he laughed.

"I didn't hear anything funny."

He focused on his chicken. "This whole subject is funny."

"Why?"

"Because it's pointless," he said. "What are you hoping to hear? Some cornball line like the two of us were meant to be? You hoping that before you gobble down your very first hot-off-the-grill chicken leg, I'll be sweeping you off of your feet, declaring my eternal love?"

She swiped a lone tear. "Why are you doing this?"

"What? You mean not being charming?" Noah stared hard at his grill, hoping to free himself from the constant images of her—laughing, crying, screaming with labor pain. He apologized for kissing her. Because what he'd done—kissing her, weaving irrational, idyllic dreams of her in his mind that occupied his every moment—he didn't feel very charming. He felt like a cad. Like a man who was taking advantage of not one but three innocent girls.

Cassie raised her chin. "In case you haven't noticed, Noah, I like kissing you back."

Noah worked his jaw, narrowed his eyes.

And in case you haven't noticed, this ain't no fancy plantation house on a rolling five-hundred-acre estate. And if that's not enough to steer you clear of me, the many members of this town's Getting Over Noah Support Group should do the trick.

Eyes narrowed, she asked, "What are you hiding?"

"What's that supposed to mean?"

"Exactly what it implies. Everything about you is

an enigma, from the ultrafeminine shrine I'm spending my nights in to this group of yours."

"For the last time—it isn't mine."

"Yours, theirs, Tiffany's—whoever. We're just talking semantics when the real issue is that all the members are screaming you can't commit, yet from what I've seen, you've committed yourself to this whole town."

That telltale muscle in his jaw popped.

"Hit a nerve, did I?"

"Chicken's done," he said, turning off the grill before stacking the meat on a clean plate. "Sorry to be a party pooper, but I've gotta hit the sack before heading to work."

"Noah, wait. I'm sorry."

"For what? Last I heard, it wasn't a crime to speak your mind."

"Yeah, but—"

"Really. The two of us—we're cool. Enjoy the grub and sun."

As WONDERFUL as the chicken had smelled, Cassie's appetite vanished along with Noah.

While Noelle and Hope snoozed on, Cassie carried the plate of drumsticks inside where she half-heartedly stole a bite of what Noah had called his World Famous Potato Salad. Lips curved into a smile at the delicious—not even a little bit healthy—taste and she longed to tell Noah he was right. His creamy concoction should've been world famous.

With the chicken and yummy potatoes safely

wrapped and in the fridge, she crept her fingers into the Ruffles bag he'd somehow smuggled into her chip-free house. Holding the potato chip to her lips, she smelled him, not the chemical-laden snack food. The salty sweat dotting the back of his T-shirt from where the worn cloth clung to his shoulders and back.

Eyeing the long, dark hall and the closed bedroom door at the end of it, she took a forbidden bite of that chip, wishing, wanting, aching for so much more.

So what was stopping her from marching right down that hall and demanding what she wanted?

Kisses. Hundreds of Noah's kisses.

Soft ones.

Hard ones.

Wicked ones licking her belly with fevered hopes and dreams. Dreams that reminded her of the fact that even though Tom hadn't loved her enough to be faithful, there were other men out there who could.

Good, honest, hardworking men like Noah who—

Cassie sharply looked away from his closed bedroom door.

Go ahead, Cass… Finish that thought.

Men like Noah who have broken so many hearts that his Victims in Love felt the need for their very own support group. A group you've already been formally enrolled in. Pretty convenient, huh?

Wrinkling the chip bag shut with a vengeance, she then stuffed it into the corner trash.

Chips were bad.

Kisses worse.

Obviously, all this junk food she'd been eating was

already having an adverse effect. The only things filling her heart and mind with these alluring what-ifs were way too many saturated fats and monotriglycerides!

"DAMMIT." Noah slapped the butt of his hand against one of the rear tractor tires. Before slitting it, Zane and his gang had painted it their trademark neon green. While Noah, Jimmy and Briggs had spent the night staking out Floyd's place, the hoodlums had been busy over at King Marshall's. The tractor was only a year old and worth thousands more than Floyd's charbroiled outbuilding. Zane and his boys needed to be taught a few manners, and it looked like the job was going to fall to Noah.

"Okay, gang," he said to Briggs and Jimmy, who had his arm in a cast. "We all know who did this, but let's go ahead and dust for prints—the tractor, those beer cans hitching a ride on the seat. Take casts of foot traffic. I want this done by the book. When you finish all that, do the same with that pile of beer cans over at Floyd's."

"Yessir." Using his good arm, Jimmy took off his hat, swiping it across the sweat beads on his forehead that'd formed in the muggy morning heat.

LATER, SHOULDERS HUNCHED, feeling like the walking dead, Noah trudged up the few steps to his porch. At least one good thing had happened that morning: Cass wasn't out there waiting for him, all sleepy-eyed and cuddly, looking like she needed a thorough kissing before spending a good eight hours spooned beside him in sleep.

Just one more reason to curse Zane and his gang of roving thugs. If it hadn't been for their escapades, he'd be back on his day shift, leaving his nights free to help Cass with the babies. No doubt she was every bit as exhausted as him. A woman shouldn't be on her own like that—especially so soon after giving birth. Oh, he knew full well she was capable of doing the whole parenting job on her own, he just wished she didn't have to.

Shoot, once this thing with Zane wrapped up, he'd give her all the help she needed—least 'til her car got fixed. From there, maybe he could take some time off. Head down to Little Rock with her just to make sure she had everything under control.

Key in the front door lock, he felt like a world-class scum.

Hadn't he just yesterday afternoon made that whole speech about how he wasn't about to go declaring his eternal love?

And how many times before that had he sworn off women altogether?

How lame his speech must've sounded, he thought, shoving open the door. At the very least, he owed Cass an apology. This damn case. It was messing with him. He wasn't thinking straight. Not that that was an excuse, just—

Aw hell, who was he trying to kid?

Inside, he closed the door behind him.

He was falling for Cass. He already loved her kids.

He wanted to watch them grow and learn. Teach them to take their first steps and ride bikes and swim. He wanted to shoo away overeager boys, tear up when the girls graduated from high school and college. And then there were the things he wanted to do with their momma. Things he ought not even think about here in the bold light of day.

Removing his utility belt, he set it on the table beside the door, then crossed the room to practically fall into his recliner.

Oh, the things he'd like to do with their momma…

Rent a secluded cabin on Beaver Lake, holding her on his lap while they watched the sunrise after they'd spent the whole night making love. He wanted to cook deliciously unhealthy foods for her, watching her big old green eyes widen in pleasure when she took her first bite of his barbecued chicken straight off of the grill. And what about his world famous potato salad? He knew all the guys from the sheriff's office and fire station loved it, but what about her? Why was it only her opinion that mattered?

Even though he and Cass hardly knew each other, technically speaking, something about the way they'd first met had forged an invisible bond he neither understood nor wanted. It just was. And apparently there wasn't a damned thing he could do about it other than bide his time until she was gone. Because even as much as he wanted to share all of those things he'd just rattled off with her and her girls, he didn't want any of them bad enough to make her an honest woman.

He couldn't marry her.

And he *wouldn't* use her.

That what you essentially did with all of those women who hate you?

Noah fiercely scowled.

No. Hell, no.

He'd loved each and every one of the women he'd been with over the years in their own special way. The difference was, they'd known up front about his failed marriage with Darla. They'd known from the start that he wasn't the marrying kind and they hadn't cared.

Cass, on the other hand, knew nothing about him except he'd helped her out of an awfully big jam one afternoon on the side of the road. She didn't know the real him. The Noah who emotionally left women before they had the chance to leave him. Because they would. Just like Darla, they would.

With an exhausted sigh, Noah pushed himself up from his recliner, figuring since the rest of the house was evidently snoozing, he might as well, too.

The shades were still drawn in his room, making it dark and cool with just a whisper of light seeping past the heavy blinds' sides and bottoms. Wincing at his aching neck and shoulders, he drew off his uniform shirt, then tugged his white T-shirt over his head.

He needed a shower, he thought, unbuttoning his pants, slipping them off, then draping them across the back of a chair. Once he had his socks off, too, and was standing there in just his boxers, he gave himself a scratch, worked the kinks out of his bum knee, then headed for the shadowy alcove housing his bed.

Yep, a couple hours of sleep and he'd be back to

his old self. He'd get Moe on the horn, tell him to rush Cass's car. Then he'd take her back to Little Rock himself, insuring for his conscience that she was safe, while at the same time insuring his own emotional safety by getting her not just out of town, but out of his house!

He eased into his bed only to hit curves.

Warm curves—lots of them!

What the—?

He drew back, fumbling for the bedside lamp. He switched it on, illuminating the Tremont girls—snug as bugs in *his* rug. Cass in the middle, a snoozing baby cozy in the crook of each arm, the TV remote hitching a ride on the lucky pale yellow afghan tucked around all three.

Noah sighed.

Great.

What was a guy to do? On the one hand, what? Hadn't he like only ten minutes earlier wished to spend the next eight hours sleeping beside her? Yet on the other, he couldn't sleep beside her *and* her babies. It was too intimate—too close to the reality a long-buried part of him had so desperately wanted.

Dammit, why had Darla ever left him?

If she hadn't, he wouldn't even be in this situation. He'd be like one of the old married guys down at the station. Guys who had inner tubes around their waists from good home cooking, and smiles on their faces while watching their kids catch touchdown passes or march with the band.

Growing up, Noah had seen nothing but the *for*

worse side of marriage, but back when he'd married Darla, he'd been young enough and dumb enough to believe his marriage would be different. He'd been naive enough to believe by sheer will he alone held the power to make it different.

Now, he knew better.

Something in him wasn't right. Maybe hearing his folks bickering while growing up had soaked in by osmosis, and now—

"Noah?" asked a sleepy female voice from the center of his bed.

He sharply looked Cass's way. "Hey. Sorry. I didn't mean to wake you."

"That's okay. Especially since we're kind of camped out in your bed."

Why?

Casting him a luminous, sleepy-eyed grin, she said, "You've got the only TV in the house where I can comfortably stretch out, and…" Eyeing the babies, she blushed. "Well…you know. I hope you don't mind. I'd planned on being out of here before you—"

"Came home."

"Yeah."

He shrugged.

Struggling to sit up, she said, "Give me just a sec, and we'll head back to our own room."

"No," he said, fingertips cool on the ivory satin sleeve of her button-up-the-front pajamas. Judging by the way they gapped atop the important parts, giving him a sideways view of her right breast, she'd been so tired when she'd finished feeding the girls that she hadn't even correctly buttoned her top.

Had she been his, he'd have buttoned it for her, skimming the backs of his fingers across full breasts that gave his daughters nourishment and him pleasure. Only Cass wasn't his, and neither were her girls, so he looked away.

"If you'd just give me a hand with these two," she said, "we'll be out of your way."

"You're not in my way, Cass," he said, somehow managing to speak past the ache that lately seemed to have taken up permanent residence in the back of his throat.

"Oh." She licked her lips. "Well, it's a big bed. If you want, why don't we just share?"

Yeah. Oh, heck yeah.

"I, ah…" He swallowed hard. "Nice as that offer sounds, I think I'll just grab a sheet from the hall closet and camp out on the couch."

Chapter Eleven

"No, Moe, that's not good at all. She needs it done sooner than that."

"That the guy fixing my car?" Cassie mouthed, strolling into the kitchen that afternoon to find Noah on the phone.

He nodded. "No, that won't work, either, but... Okay, then, catch you later."

"Bad news?" she asked, filling the kettle with water, then setting it on the stove.

"Yeah. The dealer Moe ordered your parts from is over in Tulsa. They sent the wrong color hood, so unless you want a nice red and yellow mix—"

"It's going to take a little longer." She shot him a grin.

"I expected you to be more upset."

She shrugged. "It's only time. I was supposed to be on maternity leave for a few more weeks. I figure at this point, it doesn't much matter where I spend them."

"Right."

"Of course, if you'd rather we get a room someplace else."

"Here's fine." He frowned. "You've, ah—" He waved toward her pajama top.

"Oops. Missed a button after feeding number forty-eight."

"Rough night?"

"'Round about 3:00 a.m., I was convinced I hadn't given birth to babies, but screaming demons. Nothing I did helped. Yet now, they're both snoozing away while I'm too exhausted to sleep." Joining him at the table, she asked, "How 'bout you?"

"I've had worse nights."

"Sorry about you coming home to a bed full of women."

"Shoot," he said through a devastatingly handsome lazy grin, "Don't apologize for fulfilling a long-running fantasy."

She matched his teasing smile. "Right, only in your fantasies, we were all stacked blondes?"

"Hey, I'm not choosy. Redheads'll do just fine."

Already on her way up to answer the whistling kettle's call, she bonked his head.

"Hey!"

"Is for horses. My girls and I prefer to be fantasized as auburns." She blew him a kiss.

He made a big production out of pretending to catch it, then, while she messed with her tea, he read the paper and sipped fragrant coffee.

Cassie hadn't realized how much she'd missed this kind of spirited bickering she'd once shared with her

aunt Olivia. Tom had been all business, all the time—
at least with her. Who knew what he'd been like with
his other wife? Oh sure, they'd shared plenty of ro-
mantic moments, but in retrospect, those moments
seemed almost so perfect they might have been cho-
reographed.

Hot shame enveloped her over the fact that her
whole life with Tom had been designed to make her
love him enough to toss open the family coffers.

Only the joke was on him, because she'd loved him
enough to have given him anything he'd wanted if only
he'd asked. Her aunt had always told her that loving
too fast was one of Cassie's biggest faults. She was
too quick to share her heart. Too quick to depend on
others.

Since learning of the depths of Tom's deceptions,
though, Cassie had forced herself to be just the opposite.

She'd become a one woman dynamo, depending on
no one but herself. For now that her aunt was gone,
along with her every shred of dignity, who else could
she trust? No one. At least until she'd met Noah. Only
the more attracted to his quiet strength she became, the
more put off he seemed by her.

From behind her came the rustle of the paper, then
the scraping of Noah's chair, followed by his footsteps
as he walked her way. His heat touched her back when
what she wanted was his hands. "What's for breakfast?"

Cassie's Ego on a Stick.

She swiped away a silly sentimental tear for the wish

that she'd met a man like Noah before Tom. No, not a man *like* Noah—but the real deal.

Hands gripping the edge of the counter, she asked, "Want me to make you an egg-white omelet?"

He laughed, turning to face her while leaning his back against the white tile. "I was thinking more along the lines of—uh oh, what's with the waterworks?" His touch whisper-soft, he wiped away a few stray tears. "If it means that much to you, I'll eat a dozen egg-white omelets."

"It's not that," she said, turning away from him while wishing her messy sniffle-snort was dainty like the ones in movies.

"O-okay. Did I leave the toilet seat up? Eat the last of something you had saved in the fridge?" He shook his head. "Nah, couldn't be that since I wouldn't eat your stuff even when—"

That started up a whole new bunch of tears.

"I'm sorry," he said, pulling her into the solid strength of his arms. "I was just teasing about your food. And whatever else I did, I'm sorry for that, too. Please don't cry."

"I-it's not you," she said against his chest. His wall of a chest that earlier, in the shadows of his room, she'd seen bare and in all of its muscular glory. He now wore a plain white T-shirt, making her sorry that he'd bothered to put it on. Which only made her cry all the harder, because she never used to be this needy, this hungry for a man's touch. But then again, she wasn't talking just any man, she was talking Noah, only he didn't want *her*.

That last thought made her cry all the harder.

"Think this might be some kind of pregnancy hormone thing?" Noah asked. "Want me to get hold of your doctor?"

Fisting his shirt, she shook her head.

"Okay, then, um, what seems to be the problem? Are you in pain?"

She nodded.

"What hurts? Just tell me, and I'll fix it. Well, not fix it, fix it, but you know what I mean."

She nodded.

"Great. Let's have it. Tell me where it hurts, and I'll see what I can do."

"There's n-nothing you can do." *Except hold me forever. Except after the mess Tom made of my heart, I no longer believe in forever.*

Cupping the back of her head with his big, strong hand, he pressed her even closer. "You need sleep. I'll bet that's it."

She nodded.

Yes. That was it. Hours and hours of sleep. Every minute of it spent cradled in your arms.

Scooping her up, he carried her to her bedroom, but she didn't want to go to that room with it's Sanitized For Your Protection perfection. She had that at her own house.

Here, with Noah, she wanted what was real. His dirty socks and shoes lying in the same spot where he'd taken them off. Half-full glasses of watered-down soda that'd left rings on the dresser. Comfortable bed linens smelling clean of detergent, feeling soft to her skin from years of use—his use.

"Take me to your bed," she said, knowing herself out of her mind from lack of sleep, but not caring.

Locking his gaze with hers, her lips mere inches from his, he stopped at the end of the shadowy hall. The only light spilled through the open door of her sun-flooded room.

"The girls don't seem to mind sleeping with all the lights on," she said. "But I do."

"Ah, sure." In his room, he placed her gently on the bed. He reached for the pale yellow afghan, presumably to cover her before reclaiming his previous spot on the sofa, but she sat up, circling her fingers around his wrist.

"Stay." *Hold me. Kiss me. Tell me Tom didn't steal all of me. The parts I now find myself wanting to share with you.*

Sighing, he looked at the door.

"*Please* stay. I've been told I snore, but I'm pretty sure I don't bite."

"How would I know? Can you insure you won't attack me in a fit of slumbering gnashes?"

Grinning, she urged him down beside her. "Stay."

Looking at the door, he said, "Might be dangerous."

Hand on his chin, drawing his gaze back to her, she said, "Never know, could be danger out there, too."

"True."

Sliding her fingers to the back of his head, easing them into his coarse dark hair, she drew him closer still. "Lions, tigers, juvenile delinquents. Who knows what could be lurking just beyond that door?" Her heart pounded, warning she wasn't nearly as brave as her words sounded.

She slipped her hand down to his neck. It felt tight. Beneath her wandering fingers, his muscles stood corded. "Relax," she said, gently kneading his warm, sweat-damp skin. "We've already established the fact that I don't bite."

"You established that—not me," he said, grazing her lips with his.

"Maybe you ought to investigate further."

"Maybe…" He relaxed just enough to lean into her, mounding her breasts to his chest, filling her mind and body with yearning heat, thrilling her by deepening his kiss until by mutual consent their mouths parted to explore each other still farther with their tongues. Deeper still when she groaned, and then he groaned, and was rolling onto his back, pulling her along for the ride. Deeper still when he plunged his fingers into her hair, pressing him to her, sending hot waves of sheer bliss spiraling through her. They rolled yet again, this time he landed on top, grinding against her.

"I want you so bad," he said, his voice a raspy imitation of its usual strength.

She nodded.

"That's why we have to stop."

"W-what?"

By the time she'd found the energy to make her lips form the question, he'd rolled again, only this time not only off of her, but completely off of the bed. "Noah?"

"We can't do this," he said. "I can't do this."

"Do what? All we were doing was kissing."

"Right. That's all we were doing for now, but what happens later? When your doctor gives you the green light to—you know. And we can take this where we'd evidently both like it to go? Everything'll be fine and dandy then. But what happens after that? When you see me for who I really am? A small-town sheriff with maybe a thousand bucks in the bank with no ambitions to do anything but continue down my same path. What happens when you remember where you're from and what you've given up to be here, and the novelty of small-town life wears off? What happens when you wake up one day wanting a wedding ring for yourself and a forever kind of daddy for those girls of yours? What happens then, Cass? Can you tell me?"

"Why should I?" she asked through a thick wall of tears. "Sounds to me like you've already got it all figured out." *It was just a kiss, Noah.* But even as in her mind Cassie whispered the words, her heart guiltily knew that had he but shown the slightest inclination, what they shared could have been so much more.

"Damn straight. And in case you haven't noticed, I'll tell you who else has figured it out—all those women in that damned support group. The minute they got too close, I showed them the real me and they all went running. They knew better than to get in too deep. They knew I was trouble from the word go."

"Trouble?" A bitter laugh spilled from her lips.

"Oh, so now we've gone from you being just a guy who doesn't want to commit to trouble?"

He started to say something, then clamped his lips shut. "I've gotta get out of here. Clear my head."

"No," she said, darting from the bed. Closing her hand around his forearm, she said, "This time, you're staying, and you're going to for once hear what I think your problem is."

Even in the shadows, she saw him roll his eyes. "Go ahead, make fun all you want, but you're going to listen." She dragged him back to the bed. "Sit."

"You can't be serious?"

"Sit down."

Though he sighed his annoyance, he finally did her bidding, and she sat beside him, reaching for his hand. "Wanna know what I think?"

"No. But I get the feeling you're going to tell me."

"I think you're scared."

"Scared?"

"And that because of that fear, you've decided to dump any woman you even think you might feel something for long before she gets the chance to dump you."

"I don't have to—"

"You know what else I think?" she said, climbing onto his lap when he tried to escape. "I think you keep your mother's room so nice out of guilt."

"That's just plain dumb," he said. "What do I have to feel guilty for?"

"For not being able to make her marriage better. For being a little boy and lying there night after night listening to your parents fight. Wishing, dreaming, praying you held the power to make it stop, but you didn't. And since that room was the one place in this house she most loved, you've turned it into a shrine. A shrine to your love for her. A shrine to your sorrow that the two of you weren't closer. A shrine to your current unfortunate streak with the ladies. Yet if only you'd open yourself up to trying, you might see that your failed marriage wasn't entirely your fault, but partially Darla's.''

Tensing beneath her, he said, ''Who told you about my wife?''

''Tiffany.''

''Yeah, well she likes to think she knows everything, but she doesn't.''

''Apparently, she knows more than you.''

''Meaning?''

Eyeing him, recognizing the cold fury in his eyes would be going nowhere soon, she scooted off of his lap, heading for her own room.

''Where do you think you're going?''

Hand on the doorknob, she said, ''To take a shower—a very cold one.''

''Noah?''

He woke slowly, as if running through fog.

''Noah?'' Cass said. ''You need to get up. Jimmy just called and they need you at the station.''

''Damn.'' Instantly alert—or at least trying to be, Noah bolted upright in his bed, rubbing his eyes. ''What time is it?''

"Midnight."

"Crap." He swung his legs off the bed, by rote reaching for the uniform pants he kept over his bedroom chair. He pulled them on over his boxers, wishing he didn't feel Cass's stare. Wishing he didn't care.

"Are you doing another stakeout in Floyd's field?"

"Yeah," he said reaching for his shirt. "And I should've been there, like, over an hour ago."

"Sorry. I would've wakened you, but I was—"

"It's not your problem," he said, buttoning his shirt, remembering the curve of her breasts through her only half-buttoned pajamas. His palms itched from the need to cup those breasts, testing their weight, their softness, their taste.

"I still feel bad," she said, scooping up his shoes, then pulling out a clean pair of socks for him from his top dresser drawer. Handing the bundle of shoes and socks to him, she said, "Here."

"Thanks." How had she known where he kept his socks? And these were folded into one of those tidy little origami sock balls that in over fifteen years of doing his own laundry, he never had been able to figure out.

He eyed her while sliding them on, hating himself anew for imagining her hands folding them, smoothing his aching feet, traveling up his ankles and calves and thighs and—

Finished dressing, he stood, headed for the door. "I hate running off on you like this, but…"

"It's okay," she said, crossing her arms, running her hands over her satin-covered shoulders. Trailing him down the hall, she asked, "Is what you've been doing dangerous?"

He shrugged. "Suppose it could be, but so far all Zane's pulled is pretty normal teen stuff. Problem is his frequency. Whereas most guys his age pull this kind of crap maybe once or twice during their high school careers, Zane is out doing it every night."

"And that worries you?"

"Shoot, yeah," he said, fastening his utility belt. "Little crime leads to big crime." Kind of in the same way little intimacies, like the way she was standing there looking at him, wearing nothing but those flimsy pj's and a wistful smile could turn into big intimacy if he let go of even a fraction of his will.

"Sure. I suppose I've heard that on one of those news magazine shows."

"Okay, well, guess this is it. I'm off."

"Be careful," she said, nibbling her lower lip, driving him wild with the urge to pull her into his arms for a quick yet thorough good-night kiss.

"Will do." He had his hand on the door, but staring at her in the golden glow of the living room's one meager lamp, he realized with an unfamiliar pang that for the first time in his law career, he didn't want to go to work.

He wanted to stay here.

With her.

With their girls.

"Oh—before I forget," she said, dashing off to the kitchen, giving him an all-too-enticing view of her perfectly rounded behind. "I made you something."

He stifled a groan. Great. She hadn't cooked him

something had she? Because if she had, his damned overactive conscience would demand he force it down.

"Here," she said, handing him a brown paper bag.

"Thanks," he said. "I think. What is it?"

"You'll see," she said, looking like she might have been thinking of going in for a kiss, but then changed her mind. For a split second, time stilled as she stood poised on the tips of her pretty, hot pink toes, hands outstretched as if to lean on his chest for balance. But then the moment was gone, and she was back to her normal pose, casting him that same unfathomable smile that left him even more confused.

What did she want from him?

What did he want from her?

"You'd better get going before Jimmy shows up in person," she said with an adorable sleepy-eyed wink.

"Yeah, thanks." This time when he laid his hand on the doorknob, he turned it, pushing the door open, then stepped into blessedly cool night air.

"And, Noah?"

"Yeah?"

"Be careful."

He gave her one last wave before shutting the door.

For a brief instant, he stood there stock still on the porch, taking in the nighttime chirps of crickets and spring peepers and the scents of dew-damp grass and Mrs. Kleghorn's freshly planted marigolds.

Noah squeezed his eyes closed.

How long had it been since a woman—shoot, anyone—had asked him to be careful? And for that matter, how long had it been—if ever—since he'd actually had three very good reasons to do just that?

Chapter Twelve

"Just missed 'em, Sheriff." Jimmy hooked one thumb over his belt, nodding toward the crudely formed obscene crop circle in Floyd's knee-high corn.

"You've got to be kidding me," Noah said, taking off his hat.

"Zane did this?"

"Yup. Floyd says he caught 'em red-handed, but that he wasn't fast enough to catch 'em since they were on three-wheelers."

"So then he didn't actually see Zane's face?"

"No, but he was sure it was him, along with the rest of his gang."

"So tell, me, Jimmy," Noah said, sitting on his haunches to finger the broken crop, "What do you charge kids on for this?"

His deputy shrugged. "Floyd's fit to be tied. Says this is all your fault. Well—yours and Cass's. Floyd says you haven't been worth—well, worth nothing since she came to town."

Noah added, "And Lord knows her car's been the ruination of you."

Cheeks blazing red in the portable floodlights' glare, Jimmy ducked his head.

After a few more minutes, Noah straightened to his full height before slapping on his hat. "We'd better get to work."

"Doing what? It's not like we can dust Floyd's busted crop for prints."

"No, but we might just pick up a thing or two like this." He knelt again to pick up a homemade cigarette butt. Nausea seized his stomach.

Aw, Zane, do you have any idea what you're messing with?

Needing to confirm his suspicions, Noah brought the butt to his nose. Sure enough, it hadn't been made out of ordinary tobacco, but pot.

"WHAT YOU GOT in the bag there, Sheriff?" Round about 4:00 a.m., Briggs gave Noah's lunch sack a shake.

Noah looked up from the mountain of paperwork left to tackle on his desk, eyeing the brown paper sack he'd been trying to forget. "God and Cass only know. Probably some kind of sprout and tofu sandwich, carrot sticks and a couple of raisins for dessert."

Briggs nodded.

"What can I do for you?" Noah asked.

"Nothing. That's all. Me and Jimmy were just wondering what was in the bag. Jimmy thought it might be a snake, but I—"

Noah slammed down his pen. "Jimmy honestly thought I had a snake in the bag? What? Has he been spending too much time down at Brenda's talking to Ernie?"

Briggs shrugged.

"Sounds to me like you two don't have enough to do. You get all that evidence filed against Zane?"

"Sure did."

Damn. "Then go watch Martha. Just leave me alone."

"Touchy, touchy. Babies keeping you up? 'Cause if they are, let me tell you about this surefire way my momma has to—"

"Briggs."

"Right. Just taped a new show on themed kid parties. Thinkin' of startin' up my own kid party business on the weekends. Maybe when you and Cass get hitched, I could even throw you two a themed reception. I got zoo, sports, princess and ballerina—'course those last two are pretty much interchangeable, but—"

"Briggs."

"Right. Gotcha."

Finally, Noah was once again blessedly alone, eyeing that stupid bag.

Why had Cass had to go and do a thing like that? First, her ultrasweet gesture tugged at his already aching heart. Second, the fact that she worked so hard to keep him healthy tugged him again. And third…

Aw, hell, he couldn't think of a third, so he decided to just go ahead and get his punishment over with. While eating her food was in and of itself punishment, the worst part was eating his own guilt. That night, rolling around with her on his bed—he adjusted his fly.

The incident should've never happened.

Peering into the bag's shadowy depths, he brought out a baggie of chips. What the—? Another baggie crammed with Oreos. Still another baggie holding a sandwich. Okay, here it came. Tofu City, heading his way.

But when he slipped it out to look between chemical-laden white bread slices, all he found was his favorite—bologna with mustard.

Damn, he thought, setting down the sandwich to scratch his head.

Did she have any idea how many nitrites were in a single slice of bologna? What could this artery-clog-in-a-bag mean? Was it her way of breaking up? Not that they'd ever been a formal item, but whatever the case, this couldn't be good.

He eyed the suspicious sandwich he once would've gulped in four or five bites—three on a particularly hectic night. He eyed the chips. The cookies. And found that what he was really craving was a nice dolphin-safe tuna sandwich garnished with a few sprouts.

Noah slapped his palm against his desk hard enough to inadvertently bring Briggs scrambling back into his office. "Everything all right?"

Grrr. The woman had to go.

"I'M COMING!" Cassie shouted a week later on her way to answer the door. She'd just put Hope down for a nap, but Noelle still needed a fresh diaper.

Rats, she'd been hoping to finish before Yancie from Brenda's delivered her pancakes and sausage—a vice that was getting to be a bigger blow to her ego each time Brenda herself took Cassie's order.

For some reason the woman still couldn't seem to stand her, but one of these days, Cassie planned on heading down there and straightening everything out over a large order of Tater Tots—ooh, and maybe some fried mushrooms and a hot fudge sundae.

Mouth watering, evidently caring far more about hunger than pride, Cassie peered through the door's peephole out of habit, expecting six-foot Yancie and his battered Razorback cap. Instead she saw parts of a woman standing behind a colorful flower bouquet.

Ducking, Cassie nibbled her lower lip.

In Little Rock, she'd never had uninvited company. If her neighbors ever ran out of sugar, they'd never know, since they rarely entered their kitchens!

Back to her present situation, though, she put her hand to her hair, then glanced down at her less-than-appropriate-for-guests attire of blue knit jogging shorts and Noah's Bad Bubba's T-shirt. She hadn't worn makeup in days, and who had time to brush or style hair? Shoot, since her two part-angel/part-demon babies had dropped into her lap straight from heaven, she figured she was lucky just to wash her hair!

The doorbell rang again.

This time, not knowing what else to do, not wanting to be rude to one of Noah's neighbors, Cassie pulled the door open. A tall blonde stood behind the bouquet of pink roses that upon closer inspection was decorated with twin pairs of pink teddy bears and rattles.

"Hi, I'm Kelsey," she said, "and you must be Cass." The woman's smile was as pretty as the bouquet.

Kelsey, Kelsey. Why did the name ring a bell?

"Your expression is telling me you don't have a clue who I am—a good thing when it comes to the usually fierce rumor-mill in this town. May I come in?"

"Um, sure," Cassie said, stepping aside, hoping such a friendly-looking soul wasn't an ax-murdering kidnapper in disguise.

The woman—Kelsey—made herself at home on the sofa. "Oh, these are for you," she said, holding out the flowers, which Cassie accepted, then set on the coffee table.

"Thank you. They're beautiful."

"So are you," she said with a low whistle. "Baby crud and all. Tiffany wasn't kidding when she said she had a gut feel you just might be the one."

"The one?"

"I'm sorry," Kelsey said. "Please forgive me for getting ahead of myself. I tend to forget that not everyone on the planet has lived in Riverdale all of their lives."

"T-that's okay," Cassie said, instantly adoring this woman who implied she looked not just alive but beautiful—in her current state of exhaustion.

"Anyway, to give you a quick recap on the past few

years around here, Noah and I used to be an item—at least until I made the mistake of wanting more.''

"So you're the famous Kelsey. No wonder your name sounded familiar.'' Cassie's cheeks flamed. "I was pretty out of it at the time, but if I remember correctly, Noah used your wedding gift towels to help deliver my babies.''

"Yep, I'm *that* Kelsey,'' she said with a laugh. "Owen and I just got back from our honeymoon yesterday. Camping in Colorado.'' She made a face. "I'd have rather been at some fabulous luxury resort. What a girl won't do for love—even if it means taking up fly-fishing.''

"Did you catch anything?'' Cassie asked.

"Gold nuggets.'' Fingertips on the stunning gold nugget necklace clinging to her throat, she grinned.

"Ahh, impressive for your first time out.''

"Thanks.''

"So anyway, back on topic, I don't mean to barge in, like my friend Tiff. Honestly, sometimes she can be such a busybody—like a ninety-year-old gossip in a hot thirty-year-old's body.''

"She was okay,'' Cassie said. "And she brought me a big box of chocolates—always a good thing. Would you like one? I still have tons left.''

Kelsey shook her head. "Thanks for offering, though. So like I was saying, the last thing I want to be is nosy, but when my mom told me how Noah acted around you and your girls that day at the hospital, and that word had it you were still staying with him until your car got fixed—''

"Wow," Cassie said, "This town really does have one heck of an active gossip circuit. Sounds like you know just about everything."

"Almost—at least all things not pertaining to the inner workings of one Noah Wheeler's heart."

Cassie sharply looked away from another of the blonde's brilliant smiles.

"Hit a nerve, did I?"

"No," Cassie said. "It's just that Noah and I are only friends. Nothing more. Not even a little bit more."

Still wearing that smile of hers, Kelsey nodded.

"What?"

"Methinks the lady doth protest too much."

"HEY," CASSIE SAID, greeting Noah on the porch swing later that morning. She'd long since stashed all evidence of her early-morning fix from Brenda's in the trash, and was currently telling herself she wasn't craving a double cheeseburger, Tater Tots and malt.

His scowl walked a few paces ahead of him.

"Had a tough time maneuvering through the Kleghorn's yard sale traffic, did you?"

"Grrr. Wouldn't be so bad if they only had a sale once every couple years like most normal people. But to them, yard sales are a cottage industry."

"Yeah, I like the used-car-lot flags Mr. Kleghorn strung through their lilac bushes."

Noah growled again before sitting beside her on the swing.

Glancing his way, Cassie wanted so badly to run her

fingers through his hair, easing away the frown lines creasing his forehead. From there, she'd rub his neck and shoulders, maybe finish up with a nice, long foot rub that'd have him purring in no time. She wanted to do all of that, but of course wouldn't.

Still, the thought of soon leaving, never seeing him again, never again sitting with him on this swing, the very thought left her short of breath—not to mention curiously hot and dizzy.

Or maybe that was her Tater Tot craving?

"What've you been up to?"

"A little of this and that," she said after slowing her racing pulse. "After keeping each other and me up most of the night, the babies finally fell asleep around ten this morning. I was planning on heading back to bed myself, but I had company stop by."

"Oh, boy." Covering his face with his hands, he said, "Seeing how I've got an entire town full of crazies who'd love nothing more than sticking their noses in our business, I'm not even going to venture a guess as to who it might've been."

"I didn't even know there was an *our*. But a *me* and a *you*—both quite separate entities."

Noah sighed. "You know what I mean."

She just smiled.

He was back to growling. "You gonna tell me who it was, or am I going to have to go down to Mr. Kleghorn and ask him?"

"Kelsey," Cassie said more out of a perverse desire to keep Noah all to herself awhile longer than any urge to be helpful.

"L-like as in my Kelsey?" he stammered.

"Like as in used-her-towels-to-help-me-through-labor, Kelsey. Speaking of which, I made plans to go with her downtown Monday to buy her a new set—from both of us. I thought I'd throw in a couple of china or flatware place settings, too. Do you happen to know where she and Owen were registered?"

Noah groaned.

Worlds colliding. Wasn't there a *Seinfeld* episode dealing with this whole issue?

Cass was *his*.

He wanted to lock her in the house and keep her all to himself. The last thing he wanted was any of the nuts in this town getting hold of her, filling her full of poison on the subject of him.

All because he didn't want to get married.

Well, by God, he could teach all of them a few things about marriage, because here lately—

He touched his hand to his forehead. How many times had he just thought the word marriage without a single stutter? Not many. And yet there, he'd gone and done it again!

"Noah? You all right?"

"I'm not sure," he said. "Something you put in that nitrite festival of a lunch you packed me isn't sitting all that well."

"Nitrite festival? I thought you'd enjoy all of that stuff—especially the Oreos. They're delicious!"

"Yoo-hoo! Hello, Wheelers!" Ancient Mr. and Mrs. Dickenson waved on their way by the house. Mr. Dickenson's arms were laden with yarn recently purchased at the Kleghorn's sale, while Mrs. Dickenson held Artie's leash. Artie being a twenty-one-year-old poodle with the bite of an entire school of piranhas.

"Hi, Georgia!" Cass called out with a friendly wave.

Wheelers? As in plural? *Georgia?*

Noah had known Mrs. Dickenson all his life, and here he was well into his thirties and still not allowed to call her by her first name!

"How're those adorable babies?"

"Back to being adorable now that they finally fell asleep."

Mr. Dickenson called out, "Noah, talk down at the Elks' Lodge is that you're gonna have trouble come election time if you don't get that McNally boy under control."

"Yes, sir. I'm working on it."

"The way me and my boys see it, that's not near good enough—"

"Hush." Mrs. Dickenson smacked his arm. "The man's a new daddy. He's got enough on his hands worrying about those two little ones and his new bride. He can't be expected to take on the whole world in one day."

"Yes, well—"

Artie growled at a chattering squirrel.

"Come on, Momma. Let's get our little one home." Mr. Dickenson nudged his wife on her way.

"Cassie, honey, I want to see you at next Tuesday's rose club luncheon!"

Cass started to form an objection—at least that's

what Noah hoped she'd been on the verge of doing, but it was too late. One of Riverdale's premier gossiping couples were already on their way.

"Mind telling me what that was all about?" he asked with a sideways glance.

"Sounded like a friendly neighborhood hello to me—all except for the part about your upcoming re-election. Is this Zane kid making your life a nightmare?"

"Yep." *And then there's you.*

But then was it her making life tough, or him? His own inability to relax knowing she was in the same country as him, let alone the same house. As for the times they'd shared his bed...

Nope. He wasn't going there.

Friends. All they were was friends.

And to prove that being called *The Wheelers* by Mrs. Dickenson hadn't in any way affected him, he playfully rested his arm on Cass's shoulders. "So, *Mrs. Wheeler,* what should we do today? Take the kids to the park? Grill a couple steaks?"

"Mmm, Mr. Wheeler, you know how I feel about red meat, but I suppose today I could make an exception—if you agree to grill burgers."

He gave her a squeeze. "This coming from the woman who fed me bologna? Why, Mrs. Wheeler, I must say I'm shocked."

Not half as shocked as you would be if you knew how badly I want to kiss you right now. Cassie was yet again fighting for breath. Did Noah have any idea how handsome he was? That wide smile of his, brimming with strong white teeth. His spiky-short hair eternally mussed. His deep brown eyes, and those laugh crinkles at the corners that told her no matter how serious his life became, he still knew how to celebrate the good times.

"What's going through that gorgeous head of yours, Mrs. Wheeler?" Fingers whisper-soft against her forehead, he brushed her hair back from her eyes.

I'm trying to count the number of times you've called me Mrs. Wheeler, and wondering what it might imply. "Does a girl always have to be thinking?" *Can't she just sit here enjoying the view?*

Eyes narrowed, he said, "I don't trust you when you're quiet like this."

"That makes two of us, because I don't trust you when you're teasing me like this."

"Don't trust me to what?" he said, inching closer, wielding that intoxicating grin.

To make good on that promise in your eyes.

"Not do this?" he asked, gently tugging a lock of her hair.

"Ouch."

"Wimp."

"Heck, yeah," she said. "Kiss me and make it better."

He did, and eyes closed, butterflies in her stomach easing into a gentle flutter, she melted against him, drinking in his warmth, his strength, his goodness that she'd never dreamed of ever finding in a man. She'd been the victim of Tom's lies, but why punish herself?

Why for one more second deny herself these heady pleasures?

Why? Her conscience blurted just as the kiss turned exceptionally good. *Because this guy doesn't want you. I mean, yeah, obviously, at the moment he's pretty into you, but isn't he the same guy perpetually spouting on about how the two of you will never be anything but friends? Don't you deserve more, Cassie? Don't your babies deserve more?*

"Mmm, baby…" he said. "Damn, you taste good. Suspiciously like maple syrup—maybe an Oreo. You haven't been into my stash, have you?"

"Guilty," she said. On so many counts. *Namely, wanting you.* "Noah," Cassie said, hands on his chest. "This has to stop."

"Why?"

"Aren't you the one always yammering on about how we're just friends?"

"I don't yammer."

"You also don't commit. Ringing any bells?"

"Who said anything about commitment? All I want after a crappy night of work is a nice, long kiss from my…" He sharply looked away. "I get your point."

"Exactly. What am I to you, Noah? Houseguest? Girlfriend? Playmate of the Month?"

"Never. You know you mean more to me than that."

"Do I?"

"Heck, yeah. I mean, I helped deliver your babies for pity's sake. You and those girls mean the world to me."

"Just as long as that world doesn't get too narrow?"

"What's that supposed to mean?"

"Oh, come on, Noah. Read between the lines. It means it's okay for us to kiss as long as we only do it on your terms."

"Fair enough," Noah said. "So tell me, what're your terms?"

Chapter Thirteen

Noah stared.

Cassie looked away.

"I asked you a question."

"Oh, come on." She forced a laugh. "How am I supposed to answer something like that?"

"You asked it. Answer it."

"It wasn't that kind of a question and you know it."

"What kind of question was it?"

"What kind of kiss was it?"

A damned hot one. Noah pushed himself up from the swing. "I've gotta get some rest."

"Oh no, you don't. We're going to settle this. Now."

"Give me a break," Noah said. "What do you want from me?"

A husband. Though thankfully Cassie hadn't said the thought aloud, she put her hand to her mouth—just in case.

No. No, she hardly knew Noah. What was wrong with her? Hadn't she already learned her lesson with Tom? Hadn't he taught her only too well what havoc misplaced trust played upon her heart? Why would she even think of getting herself into another set of lifelong vows? Especially with a guy who every girl in town save for her knew had no intention of ever marrying again?

"Cass?" Sitting back beside her on the swing, he said, "What do you want from me?"

"Nothing. I'm sorry I ever brought it up."

"No. I started this by kissing you. It's only logical for you to now wonder where things stand between us."

Nowhere.

A fact which she'd known all along. So why, since the fact wasn't anything new, did it hurt so bad to admit? Even if only to herself? "I just want us to be friends, okay?"

He nodded, reached to her lap to take her hands into his. "Friends sounds good."

No, not good—*safe.*

"As, um, my friend, care to join me in a nap before the girls wake up?"

FIVE MINUTES LATER, lying beside Noah on his big bed, Cassie sighed.

"What was that for?" he asked.

"For my body being bone weary, but my brain being wide-awake."

"Come here." Tugging her closer, he rested his hand in the hollow of her hip, awakening places Cassie thought her body had temporarily closed for repairs.

"Um, excuse me," she said, "but isn't closeness a direct violation of the friendship rule?"

"Only if you're under the age of fourteen."

"Oh."

"Roll over."

"Why?"

"You ask too many questions. Can't you just for once do as I ask?"

"Not without a valid reason."

"Okay, then, how about this, because we'll both be more comfortable." Easing her over, he cinched her backside to his front, spooning her with his hand warming her belly, his arm forming a pillow for her head. He was right. This was comfy. Dangerously comfy. And for once, she didn't care.

"WHAT ARE YOU DOING?" Cassie asked, strolling sleepy-eyed into the kitchen. Afternoon sun slanted through the windows, bathing Noah and the babies in a golden glow. He held a girl in each of his arms, and on the table a thick book of nursery rhymes was held open by twin cans of baked beans.

"What's it look like I'm doing? These kiddos've been watching too much TV," he said with a laugh. "Time for them to get some book smarts."

The sight of him holding her two girls brought instant tears. How was she supposed to want him to be nothing more than a friend, when everything about him screamed great husband and father? Was it pregnancy hormones bringing on this nesting instinct? Or was it something more?

Swallowing hard, she said, "How are they doing?"

"Straight As. How else would our kids be other than brilliant?"

"You say that a lot, you know," she said, taking Hope from his arms.

"What?"

"That the babies are *ours*. Do you really feel that way?"

He took a long time to answer. "You know, I do. Just like I know I probably sound like a major nutcase for even saying something like this, but having that front row seat to see them come into the world—actually helping them into the world, it's made me feel kind of proprietary about them." He shrugged. "Guess it's a finders-keepers sort of guy thing."

She smiled on the outside, but on the inside came crushing sadness for the way things might've been if only each of them in their own highly personal ways weren't so afraid to trust. Because Noah refused to open up, she could only guess at the pain lining his heart.

Her own pain, now that was something she was intimately acquainted with.

And here was Noah, so different from Tom, so very good. Caring for her and her girls not in flashy ways, but in genuine little ways that showed more about his character in one tucked blanket or tender diaper change than any of the fancy cars or jewels her husband had bought her with her own money.

She longed to fling her arms around Noah, kissing him while at the same time showing him in a hundred different ways that everything between them would always be all right. But she could no more guarantee that than she could be sure he'd win his reelection by a landslide. Some things were out of her control, and sadly, their relationship—or lack thereof—was one of them.

"Oh, I forgot to tell you," he said. "Moe called me down at the station about your car. It'll be ready Monday morning."

"Monday, huh? There goes my shopping trip with Kelsey."

"Is that so bad? What's the matter? I thought you'd be thrilled, but you look like you're—"

"I'm just sleepy, okay?" She faked a yawn. Forcing a chipper tone, she then added, "Did you hear that, sweetie? Monday we'll be going home."

"Would you rather stay on 'til Tuesday?" Noah asked. "You and Kelsey could do your girl thing. Plus, I've got to be in court Monday, meaning I can't drive you unless you want to get a late start. Tuesday would probably just be better all around."

"That's okay," she said. "I'll go with the limo company as I'd originally planned."

"I thought we'd been over this. *I* want to take you home."

"Noah…" She sighed. "For the last time, as much as I've appreciated your help over the past weeks, you're not in any way beholden to me. If anything, I owe you."

"Okay then, if you won't let me drive you home, then at least let Jimmy do it."

"Jimmy? The same Jimmy who crashed my car?"

"Aside from that one incident, he's got a spotless driving record. I think getting behind the wheel of your snazzy car just got him a little too excited. Please, Cass. You just said you owed me. I trust Jimmy. If you insist on going home Monday, he's your man."

No, Noah. You're my man. If only we could both learn to trust enough to let each other in.

But seeing how the likelihood of that happening was zilch, Cassie resigned herself to taking a very long drive with a very young deputy she hoped had learned his lesson on the evils of fast driving!

The phone rang.

"Want me to get it?" Cassie asked.

"Nah, I've been waiting on the results of some fingerprints I sent off. That's probably Briggs." On his way to the phone, Noah passed her the babies, then took the receiver. "Hello?"

"Hey, Sheriff."

"Hey yourself, Cratchett." Cratchett was usually one of the night shift guys, who'd recently been pinch-hitting for him on the day shift. "You get those fingerprint reports?"

"No, but I did just get a call from Delores down at Dollar General."

"Oh?"

"She said she just caught three teenaged girls shoplifting chocolate Santas from out of her sale bin, but that when she confronted them, they ran off, and were too quick for her to catch them."

Noah groaned, leaning the back of his head against

the wall with a thud. "She at least made a positive ID, right?"

"Yeah. She said she's pretty sure if she saw 'em again she could pick them out of a lineup."

"Well, seeing how it's not likely we're going to have a lineup round here, why don't you get hold of Barbara Jenson—the high school librarian, then see if she can get you last year's yearbook. Maybe Delores can spot them in there."

"Good thinkin', Sheriff."

Yep, that's why they pay me the big bucks. "Let me know if you find out anything more."

"Will do."

LATER THAT AFTERNOON, Noah was just leaving the station after having helped Barbara Jenson flip through yearbooks—she'd refused to work with anyone but him—when he had the misfortune of literally running into Nurse Helen.

"Excuse me," she said, finally looking up after having been digging through her purse. "Oh—it's you."

"Brrr," Noah said. "Who turned on the snow?"

"Looked in the mirror lately?"

Noah hardened his jaw. If he'd ever needed confirmation of his decision to steer clear of all women, Nurse Helen was it. "Why do you hate me?" he asked, not even sure why.

She laughed. "You played me, Noah."

"Played you?"

She looked away. "That's what I said. Need to stop by the hospital to clean out your ears?"

He sighed. "How did I play you?"

"Let's see," she said, one hand on her hip, the other on her chin. "There was that time you asked me to be your date to the elementary school carnival."

"Yeah, so? I was working the child fingerprint booth, and thought you might want to come along."

She rolled her eyes. "Oh please, like you didn't deliberately ask me there so that I could see how great you are with kids?"

"Um—no."

"All right then, how about all those times you said you preferred staying in to double dating with Munchie and Connie?"

"You know your friend Connie's laugh gives me hives."

"Oh, it does not," she said with a sour look. "That's not even medically possible. The way I saw it, you wanted to stay home watching movies all those nights to try us out as a comfortably married couple."

Now Noah was rolling his eyes. "That's the craziest thing I've ever heard. We were watching movies and knocking back a few pizza rolls and chips. How do you get trying on marriage out of that?"

"You're impossible," she said. "I can't fathom what Cassie sees in you."

"Who says she sees anything? Unlike you, she doesn't think about nothing all day but the almighty institution of marriage. And also unlike you, she doesn't have a problem with just being friends."

"Friends? That's what you think you are?" Now Helen was back to laughing.

Noah shook his head in disgust. "I'm outta here."

"Good!" she shouted after him as he climbed into his county-issued ride. "I wouldn't want my opinion of you raised by thinking you were actually capable of sticking around long enough to complete a conversation!"

"WE SHOULDN'T BE IN HERE," Cassie said Saturday night in Noah's bed, snug with Hope asleep in her arms, Noah beside her, cradling Noelle.

Outside, rain pelted the windows, and after occasional cracks of lightning, thunder rolled.

"Why not?" he asked, using the remote to change the TV channel. Because from his point of view, after that nasty run-in with Nurse Helen, there wasn't anyplace in the world he'd rather be. He landed on a show with lots of fog, flickering lights and eerie music. "You like ghost shows?"

She scrunched her nose. "I'm not sure. It's been a while since I've seen one."

"You're in for a treat."

"Shouldn't you be sleeping?"

He shrugged. "I got enough sleep this afternoon." He reached over to tug a lock of his *friend*'s hair. "Besides, you and the girls are short-timers. I want to spend all the time with you I can."

"That's sweet, Noah, but not necessary."

"What if I told you I'm not doing it to be sweet, but selfish?" With the backs of his fingers, he grazed her cheek.

"I'd tell you you definitely need sleep because you've started talking crazy."

For the longest time he just looked at her, and while a commercial for The Clapper came and went, Cassie lost herself in Noah's deep brown gaze. If only they could freeze themselves in this perfect moment in time. No conflicts, no worries, just the four of them, content together, sheltered from so many different storms.

The eerie ghost-show music came back on, and Noah tucked Noelle sitting upright against his chest. "There," he said, "Now you can see all the action. Kids love ghost shows."

The moment had passed, save for the thick lump of wondering lodged at the back of Cassie's throat.

After she'd found out about Tom's deceptions, she'd been so quick in assuming she'd never open her heart again. But what if she'd been too hasty? What if the right man made all the difference? Sure, she'd long ago proven herself capable of doing most everything on her own, but did she want to anymore? Wouldn't it be much more fun sharing her life? Her babies' lives?

Peering her way, Noah said, "You need to sit Munchkin Number Two up to see the show. Look at all she's missing." On TV, a transparent woman wearing a filmy white dress floated down the curved staircase of an antebellum home.

"Mm-hmm, this is sending quite an educational message."

"Darn straight. It's teaching them to never stay in

those creepy old musty-smelling bed-and-breakfasts when they go on vacation. Always go for the nice, safe, generic Best Western.'' He crowned his speech with a quick kiss to Noelle's curls.

Cassie rolled her eyes, and after a few more minutes of watching the paralyzingly slow ghost show, she was blinking her eyes in an effort to stay awake. But it was no use. The rhythm of the rain had grabbed hold of her and there was nothing she could do other than snuggle already-sleeping Hope closer before resting her own head on Noah's strong shoulder.

AT ELEVEN, Noah's alarm buzzed.

Out of habit, he started to reach for it, but his arm wouldn't budge. He looked down to see an angel peering up at him. Noelle, her blue eyes wide, and looking much too old for her supposedly young soul.

''Why didn't you tell me you weren't sleepy?'' he whispered after freeing his arm to squelch the alarm. ''I'm always up for a party with a beautiful girl.'' He inched her higher on his chest, wondering at the intensity of her stare.

What was she thinking? Did she know who he was? Would she miss him when they were gone?

''I'm going to miss you.'' The tightness in his chest telling him just how much surprised even him.

Above the still-falling rain, she made a cute gurgling sound he'd have liked to assume meant that, yes, she would very much miss him, but it was probably nothing more than escaping gas.

Noah glanced at his namesake's momma. At the impossible beauty radiating from her even in sleep. She was way out of his league. Her skin had this pampered glow, her hair a luster of the kind he'd never before seen. And even if all of those points weren't major issues, his hang-up with relationships was.

Say Cass was on her own, if they'd been dating, that would be one thing. But her having the girls transformed dating into a character debate. He wouldn't offer this woman anything less than marriage, and seeing how he wasn't ever planning on marrying again, that pretty much stopped the whole issue dead in its tracks.

Noelle graced him with another gurgle.

"Sorry, squirt," he said, kissing her again on her forehead before giving her an extra firm hug, hoping she'd carry it with her for a lifetime, like he knew he would the feel and smell of her and her sister. How it was possible, he wasn't sure, but in the short time they'd been together, he'd grown to love these two girls.

Love them as if they truly were his own.

Shoot, who was he trying to kid?

He'd loved those two from the moment he'd first set eyes on them. As for their momma... He wasn't sure how he felt besides alternating between wanting her to leave town as soon as possible and never wanting to let her go.

He traced the fine hairs on Cass's forearm.

Finding her skin chilled, he edged off of the bed, nestling Noelle beside her before drawing the fallen afghan over all three of his girls.

Noelle's eyelids were already drooping, so he crept

away from the cozy threesome, spirits momentarily buoyed that he still had one more day and night with them before he'd most likely never see any of them again.

Chapter Fourteen

They're gone.

Monday morning, Noah sat perched on the edge of a marble bench in the bustling county courthouse hall. Though men and women teemed around him, never had he felt so alone.

It was ten-thirty in the morning, and Jimmy was supposed to have picked Cass up at the house by ten, loading her car straight onto the trailer, then driving her and the babies home without passing *Go*.

The plan was simple. All contingencies accounted for. So why was it Noah was having such a tough time finding air?

He loosened his shirt collar, but it didn't help.

He knew damn well nothing would help other than seeing his girls again. Only that wouldn't do him any good either seeing how he'd only want to see them again and again after that.

After spending Sunday afternoon barbecuing and laughing and kissing, they'd fallen asleep in his bed again—the four of them—feeling more like a family than he ever had in his life. Knowing it'd hurt too bad to give them a proper goodbye, he'd kissed all three of them one last time on their foreheads, breathing in their smells, their very essences that would, God willing, stay with him a lifetime, since he couldn't have the real thing.

Then, tears stinging his damned cowardly eyes, he'd crept out of the house, locking the door behind him, never looking back. Not because he didn't want to, but because if he had, he'd have run back inside and never come out again.

Nope. Leaving them was the right thing.

They deserved better than some coward like him who wouldn't know what to do with the word commitment if it jumped up and bit him on the—

"Here's your coffee, Sheriff." Briggs handed him a paper cup.

"Thanks."

"You look like shi—"

"Who asked you?"

"Just thought I'd point it out. Bummed about her leaving, huh?"

Noah shrugged.

"Why don't you ask her to stay?"

"You mean to stick around and date me? Nah," he said, thumping the back of his head against the polished marble wall. "Dating single moms has never been my thing. Bad karma."

"I don't know," Briggs said, sipping at his own coffee. "You ever thought about more?"

"What kinda more?"

"You know. Marrying her."

"Shouldn't we be heading into court?"

"The last case hasn't even wrapped up."

"Yeah, well I'll tell you what is wrapped up—this conversation."

"SORRY I'M SO LATE," Kelsey said, leaning over to unlock the passenger door of her mossy green Sebring convertible. "Automatic locks got stuck. I had a devil of a time opening the doors."

"That's okay," Cassie said, climbing in. "Your mom and I got to know each other better while we were waiting."

"She's been so excited about watching your babies," Kelsey said, putting the car into gear and zooming down the street. "Here I've barely been married two weeks and she's already piling on the pressure for me and Owen to get started on our family."

"She sure adores Sammy."

"We all do. I swear, sometimes I think Noah was more upset about losing her than he was me. She's a real sweetheart—loves him. All kids do. Probably because he's such a child himself."

"Ouch."

"Sorry," Kelsey said, making a left turn. "As happy as I am with Owen, sometimes I still can't get over what a big baby Noah is when it comes to commitment."

"Oh?"

"I mean, looking back on it, it's for the best we didn't get hitched. Now that I see what true love is all about—what I share with Owen—I'd never want to go back. Sometimes I have to pinch myself to believe I found him."

Stopped for a red light, Kelsey fluffed her bangs while looking in the rearview mirror. "I used to laugh at people who claimed to have found love at first sight, but *wham.* That's exactly what happened with us. From the minute I first laid eyes on Owen, I knew he was the one."

"For real?"

"Absolutely. We met at this church thing I hadn't even wanted to go to, but my mother dragged me along. So there I was, standing in line for roast beef and instant mashed potatoes, when I dropped my fork." The light turned green and she turned the car right. "I knelt to pick it up, and on the way bumped heads with Owen. He kissed the bump. I'd known him forever as a casual acquaintance, but something about that moment, about the way he was so tender in making sure I was all right." Glancing Cassie's way, she held her hand over her heart. "That was it. From that moment on, we were inseparable. Kind of like you and Noah after the night he helped deliver Noelle and Hope."

Cassie gulped. "Have we been together so much that people have actually noticed?"

"Uh, yeah. Come on, tell me true," Kelsey said, stopping for another light. "I promise to keep it just between us girls. Do you like him?"

"Of course I like him. Even though we've only known each other a couple of weeks, I feel like we've been friends forever."

"*Friends,* huh? That glow that comes over you whenever I mention his name doesn't look much like friendship to me. And from what I've heard, he's positively smitten with you and your girls."

"No," Cassie said. "No, we're definitely just friends. That's why I'm going home."

"Because you've fallen for him and can't bear the pain of sticking around if the feelings aren't mutual?"

Cassie shot Kelsey a look she hoped conveyed her wish that the subject be dropped. The fact that her feelings for Noah were so transparent was mortifying.

"I've seen the way he looks at you, Cassie. I've seen the way he kisses you, too, and believe me, speaking as the current world record holder for the longest time spent dating the infamous Noah Wheeler, I can assure you, he never once kissed me with such—what's the word?" she said, making another left. "Heat. Nah, that kiss yesterday afternoon wasn't just heat, but fire. Trust me, the guy's a goner for you."

"So you were in the yard? Watching?"

"Just during the high points. Mom sent me and Owen over with a fruit salad for you two. She has a view of Noah's backyard through her laundry room window and during the rinse cycle she saw the two of you out barbecuing."

Cassie groaned, covered her face with her hands.

Kelsey pulled into The Dent Doctor's parking lot. "You don't have anything to be embarrassed about," she said, easing down Cassie's left hand. "Noah's essentially a great guy—though not every misty-eyed member of our group agrees. I've tried explaining to the girls how his folks never got along all that well, and how he thought in his own marriage he could do things right, but when he and Darla split—you do know about his ex-wife, don't you?''

Fighting back tears, Cassie nodded.

''Well, ever since they fell apart, he's put up this wall that we never thought anyone would be able to break down. At least until he met you. Now…'' She had her hand on her door handle. ''Now, I'm thinking the two of you tying the knot is no longer in your control.''

''Right,'' Cassie said with a bitter laugh. ''Mind telling me whose hands it's in?''

''Simple,'' Kelsey said with a broad smile. ''Fate.''

CASSIE FELT STRANGE once again being behind the wheel of her car. It looked brand-new, smelled brand-new, and if it weren't for her smaller belly, she could have almost talked herself into believing her days in Riverdale had been nothing more than a dream, and that she didn't feel brand-new herself. But she did, and no amount of dreaming could change that—as much as it hurt, she wouldn't want it to.

If nothing else, she owed Noah a thank-you for teaching her that maybe her life could be different— better. She didn't have to stay locked in that cage she'd built around herself since learning of Tom's deception.

Pulling into the driveway of the house now more familiar than her own, Cassie turned off the engine and rested her forehead against the steering wheel.

How was she going to leave this place? This man?

Saying goodbye to Kelsey had already been surprisingly hard, but leaving what had become her home without even having given Noah a proper goodbye...

Jimmy, parked at the curb with Noah's Suburban, the trailer for her car already hitched behind, gave her a jaunty wave. "Hey there, Ms. Tremont."

"Hey, Jimmy."

He took off his NASCAR ballcap and used it to wipe the sweat from his brow. "Your car run all right?"

"Like new."

His shoulders slumped. "I'm really sorry 'bout what happened. I never meant to—"

"I know," she said, patting his upper arm. "And anyway, it's fixed now, so no more worries, okay?"

"Sure. If you'll trust me with her one last time, I'll drive her up on the trailer." His big, goofy grin brightened her mood.

"Sure," she said, dangling her keys. "Go for it— only this time, I don't want to see you going much over three miles per hour."

"Gotcha," he said with a wink, already rushing toward her car.

Kelsey's mom, Evelyn, came out the front door. "Is it that time already?"

"Afraid so," Cassie said, crossing the small lawn to climb the few porch stairs.

"I wish you could stay longer. I thought you didn't have to be back at your firm for weeks yet?"

"I don't," Cassie said, stepping into the woman's outstretched arms for a warm hug the likes of which she hadn't received since before her aunt died. "But I can't stay here any longer," she said, easing back not because she wanted to, but because she had to. "I can't keep taking advantage of Noah's hospitality."

"He likes having you here."

Cassie folded her arms, biting her lower lip to keep from crying as she watched Jimmy load her car onto the trailer.

"I've known Noah his whole life, Cassie. He's a good man. Hurting, confused, but at the core, good. All it would take is a nudge from a girl like you to bring him back to life."

"Seems like he leads a swell life to me. Plenty of action and adventure at work. More dates than he knows what to do with."

"That isn't living," Evelyn said with a firm shake of her head. "Not to a man like Noah. His whole life, that boy's been searching for a home. Bless her, his mother tried, but I don't think her heart was ever really into it. She kept pretty much to herself, never opened up to any of us. Even at the occasional school function we'd all meet up at, we knew things weren't quite right between her and Noah's daddy."

"They spent a lot of time arguing?"

"At first. When Noah was little. But then once he grew older, they didn't talk much at all. Noah was always real friendly. Oh sure, he went through the usual rebellious stage, but with all of our help, he came out strong."

"I appreciate you telling me all of this, Evelyn, but seeing as I'm leaving, I don't understand why."

Evelyn pulled her into another hug. "Because Noah won't. But mostly, because in order for you to make an informed decision, you need to know."

"A decision about what? I'm leaving. The babies are all packed save for a few bottles and diapers and wipes."

"You're right." The older woman sighed. "You're leaving, and I've turned into the meddlesome old woman I've always hoped I'd never become." Still holding Cassie tight, she said, "Please don't be a stranger. Know that if you ever need anything—anything at all, you'll always find shelter here."

"Ready, Ms. Tremont?" Jimmy shouted from the curb.

Swiping at a few tears, Cassie nodded, thinking herself silly for getting so emotional over leaving people she hardly knew.

Evelyn unabashedly sniffed, too. "I was thinking maybe Kelsey and I would head to Little Rock soon for a shopping trip. You gave her your phone number, right?"

Cassie nodded.

"All right, then, seeing how I'm just sure she'll be needing maternity clothes any day now, we'll probably be visiting you in a couple of weeks."

"She never told me she was expecting," Cassie said.

"She's not." Evelyn winked. "But a mother can dream, can't she?"

On that note, with Cassie still grinning, Evelyn left, and while Jimmy finished securing her car to the trailer, Cassie wandered through Noah's house on a halfhearted search for anything she'd left behind.

A pink bootie rested beside the toaster.

A pink Velcro hair bow beside the bathroom sink.

And there, in Noah's bed, was her heart.

Squeezing her eyes closed tight, she recalled the laughing, talking, tickling…kissing.

What had it all meant? Why was she so afraid that she'd never again feel even half as alive?

She owed those babies nestled sound asleep in their carriers all of herself. But how could she give them that when just by walking out Noah's front door, she was so afraid of leaving the best of herself behind?

Yes, she was perfectly capable of raising Noelle and Hope all by herself, but these past few days had been like a menu for her future. Daily Special 1: Go it alone as planned. Daily Special 2: Go it with Noah, and his cozy, wonderful home with its worn carpet and furniture and cabinets stocked full of forbidden food. His wild friends and even wilder work schedule. His smile, and those crinkles at the corners of his warm brown eyes. His laughs and kisses and magical knack for always making her feel safe and secure and…loved.

Loved?

Goose bumps dotted her arms. To compensate for suddenly weak knees, she sat on the edge of the bed.

Was it possible that this absolute refusal for her feet to move from this room was love?

She'd thought she'd been in love with Tom, but look how that had turned out, and she'd known him years before they'd married. Noah, she'd known days, yet felt as if she'd known him lifetimes. And here she was on the verge of leaving him without so much as a formal goodbye.

If nothing else, he deserved thanks for having safely seen her through the delivery of her babies.

"Ms. Tremont?!" Jimmy called, presumably from the front door. "I'm ready whenever you are. Looks like it might storm, so if we want to beat the rain, we should get a move on."

Her heart pounded.

Sitting here in this room, for the first time in months Cassie felt wanted—maybe even needed. Oh sure, not in any practical sense, but make no mistake, Noah needed her to remind him that no matter what kind of dysfunctional family he'd been raised in, no matter that his first wife had left him, no matter what the members of that wretched support group thought, to Cassie's way of thinking, he was a wonderful man. Just like she was making a conscious decision to no longer be Tom's victim, Noah could do the same by deciding he's no longer the type of man who steered clear of commitments.

They both deserved fresh starts. Together.

But in order to do that, she had to be here, in Riverdale. She had to at least stick around long enough to discover if there was even a chance of him realizing he loved her as much as she now knew she loved him.

"Ms. Tremont?" Jimmy called. "I left the truck running. You ready?"

Shoulders straight, chin high, Cassie swiped what she hoped would be the last of sad or frightened tears.

From now on, if Noah would have her, there'd be nothing but happy tears for the rest of her life.

In the living room, overcome with a remarkable sense of calm that in staying, she was making the right decision, Cassie said, "Thanks so much for all of your trouble, Jimmy. But it looks like I'll be sticking around."

As NOAH WALKED slump-shouldered out of the courthouse, his mood went from bad to worse when he was blindsided by a wall of muggy heat the likes of which usually ushered in a storm. No wonder his knee had been bellyaching all damned day. And what a day it'd been.

He'd had to testify in a domestic abuse case, and even though Heather Clement's husband, Vince, would be having a nice long vacation behind bars to think about what he'd done, no one had really come out a winner.

Not the two scared kids left in the care of their grandmother out in the cold, marble courtroom hall, quietly coloring while inside the courtroom their father was taken into police custody. Not Heather, whom Noah had gone to high school with, and had known as a vivacious, fun-loving science whiz who'd taken her science fair project all the way to nationals in her senior year. Vince's repeated abuse had reduced her to a hollow shell of her former self.

She deserved so much better than a creep like that. So what'd happened? What happened to turn a guy who'd always seemed like a decent, hardworking man into a wife-beating monster? Or had he always been that way, only Noah had been too blind too see it?

He shook his head, climbing into his city-owned ride.

That question, along with so many others he faced on a daily basis, he figured might never be answered. Just like his question of why he couldn't shake the feeling that in letting Cass and her babies go, he was making the worst decision of his life.

Yeah, right, he thought, putting the Blazer in gear and pulling onto Cherry Street. It might be the worst decision for him, but not for Cass. Not for her precious twins.

All three of those girls deserved better than him.

Just as fat raindrops splattered his windshield, filling the Blazer with the scent of cool water meeting parched blacktop, he realized that Heather and Vince's case was just one more shining example proving marriage didn't work.

And yeah, their case might be extreme, but then maybe that was why fate had decided to make their case coincide with Cass's leaving. To show him that letting her go was a good thing—the only thing he could possibly do.

He was heading home for some shut-eye before that night's shift when he got word of a suspected drunk driver out on the highway south of town. With another weary sigh, Noah waited for an oncoming car to pass, then did a U-turn and gunned it, turning on his windshield wipers right after his siren.

WOULD THIS DAY never end?

Sure enough, Noah rode up on the drunk driver ten

miles outside of town. He was belligerent and barely able to walk—let alone drive—in the pouring rain. His blood alcohol read .17.

By the time Noah loaded the guy up, got him processed, called one of Moe's men out to deal with the drunk's green Ford Ranger, then handled a minor fender bender back in town, Noah was too tired for even the short drive to his house, so he crashed on the lumpy sofa in the station's break room.

What was the point in going home? It'd only hurt.

Round nine that night, the rain thankfully over, he'd headed out to Zane's, planning on chatting with the kid before his nightly party. Trouble was, Zane wasn't home, leaving Noah stuck in an ugly verbal sparring match with his old man who reeked of sweat, stale beer and self-righteousness.

It was 1:00 a.m. by the time Noah and Briggs stumbled across the aftermath of Zane's latest escapade—a robbery at the town's only liquor store.

The only good thing about Zane was that he was messy, leaving prints galore and a bonus prize of a surveillance tape. *Surprise, you little creep. You're on* Candid Camera. He and his partner had both worn paper bags over their heads, but by the end of the booze fest, Zane's had fallen off, giving a clear shot of the back of his head.

Just as soon as they found him, Zane was going down. The time for softhearted intervention had passed. With this robbery, he'd gotten himself into serious trouble.

By eight in the morning, when there was still no sign of Zane, or his usual posse, Noah cried uncle—at least to the lethargy taking over his body.

It was time to go home.

Like Zane, he couldn't hide forever. And he sure couldn't stay awake forever—no matter how bad climbing into his bed that would most likely still smell of Cass's perfume was gonna hurt.

But then a curious thing happened. For when Noah finally pulled into his drive, it was to snuggle his big, ugly SUV right up alongside Cass's sleek yellow convertible.

For a split-second, his spirits soared along with the new day's brilliant sun, only to stumble upon the realization that if she hadn't left, something must be wrong with either her or the babies.

Why hadn't she called him? he thought, heart pounding, instantly awake as he jumped an azalea bush, taking a short cut to the front porch.

Storming inside, he started to shout Cass's name, but then worried he'd wake the babies. A quick visual inspection told him that far from there being anything wrong in his house, nothing had ever been more right.

"Good morning," Cass said, her beautiful face still sleepy-eyed from what had presumably been her own rough night. She stood behind the stove, flipping savory-smelling sausage patties. Her long hair down. Wild and sexy from having done nothing to it at all. Her satiny pink flowered nightgown accentuated her every curve—most notably, full breasts he wanted pressed against his chest—now.

"Seeing you…" Noah said, frozen on the kitchen's threshold, "…smelling that sausage, I'd say what we have here is a damned sight more than a good morning. More like *grrreat*."

"Mmm…" Laughing, scooping the meat out of the pan to lay it on a paper-towel-lined plate, she said, "I love it when you go all Tony the Tiger on me."

And I love—nope. Couldn't even think it, let alone say it. What he felt for her right now was certainly more than friendship, but it wasn't the "L" word, either. Every woman in town knew he wasn't capable of that. "Not that I'm complaining," he said once his pulse slowed to normal, "but what are you doing here? Everything all right?"

She nodded.

"When Jimmy didn't show up last night, I thought—"

"I'm sorry," she said. "We were getting a pretty late start anyway, and he looked so tired, that I told him he should go home and get some rest. I hope you don't mind."

Heck yeah, he minded, but then he looked at her. At the sunlight glinting sparks off of her long, gorgeous hair. At her luminous eyes that had this knack for making him forget everything but her. "Nah," he said. "You were probably right. Jimmy, along with the rest of us all need some serious shut-eye."

"Guess with my night-owl crew, though," Cass said, "even if you were here for a full night, you wouldn't get much rest.'' Refusing to meet his gaze, she fiddled with the spatula while the last remaining sausage patty sizzled.

"Cass?'' Once again capable of movement, he went to her, easing his hands about her waist, losing himself in the smell of her perfume and expensive shampoo and lotion. Not to mention the sausage she'd broken her every healthy-food rule to prepare just for him. And then there was her satiny gown—the one looking and feeling so damned good with her pressed up against him, that he'd just as soon tug his shirt off, feeling her curves bound in cool, slick satin against nothing but his bare skin. "Why are you still here?''

"I…'' Her breath hitched, and she clung to him before pushing away. Staring up at him through tear-filled, jade-green pools, she said, "I'm here because no matter how crazy it sounds, I love you, Noah. I love everything about you from your laugh to your unhealthy foods to the way you take care of me and my babies. Will you please marry me, Noah?'' She shyly looked down, then back up. "I mean, will you please marry *us?*''

Chapter Fifteen

Standing there, waiting for Noah's answer, Cassie's heart beat so fast she feared she might be having some kind of attack.

What had she done?

She'd never meant to blurt out all of her feelings like that, let alone just come right out and ask him to marry her. But now that she had, she wasn't sorry. She'd spoken what was in her mind and heart. The truth.

Reaching for his hands, she gave him an excited squeeze. "I don't think we'll want a big wedding. You and the girls are my only family. Just something quiet with a few of our friends. We can have it right here if you'd like. Maybe on the deck, and for the reception you can get one of your friends to barbecue. I'd ask you, but as the groom, you'll be busy."

"Cass…"

"Wait—" Releasing him, she spun off to the far end of the counter where there was a notepad and pen beside the wall-mounted phone. "Okay, talk now. I'm

so excited, I just know we'll lose some great ideas if
I don't jot them down.''

He said nothing.

Just stood there.

Staring.

''Noah? Is everything all right? We can talk about
all of this later if you want.'' Going to him, pressing
her palms to his strong chest, she said, ''Your heart's
beating a mile a minute. Maybe before we talk anymore about the wedding, you ought to grab a nap.''

''I don't need a nap,'' he said, taking the pad and
pencil from her to set them on the counter.

''Then what's wrong?''

When he still said nothing, just stood there with that
muscle in his jaw popping—the same one that popped
whenever he was upset or—taking a step back, she
covered her mouth with her hands.

Had she just fallen off the turnip truck?

Here she was yammering about their wedding when
look at him... Lips pressed tight, normally warm gaze
distant and cold. He wasn't sharing in her excitement,
because he wasn't excited. Oh, he was sick all right,
but not physically. He was sick over her impromptu
proposal—not to mention the fact that he evidently
couldn't think of a kind way to turn her down, so instead he was just standing there letting his silence do
the talking.

Shaking her head, crying, trembling, wanting to do
all of it in blessed private, she dashed down the hall
to her room.

''**Cass, wait!**'' Noah shouted.

She hastily shut the door.

Inside, bathed in warm morning sun, Noelle and Hope contentedly snoozed on, blissfully unaware that for the second time in their lives, their daddy had abandoned them.

No. That wasn't fair to Noah.

As much as his rejection hurt, she'd set herself up for this fall. He'd never been anything but honest with her, telling her right up front practically from their very first kiss that whatever the two of them shared, it would never go further. She'd been the one overcome with this ridiculous notion of love. And now she'd be the one left once again picking up the broken pieces of her heart.

"Cass?" Noah said, his voice muffled outside her door. "Let me in."

"No."

"Come on, baby. We have to talk."

She closed her eyes, hurt all the more by his gentle tone. Wanting to hate him, yet even now, in the face of his rejection, somehow loving him more. And that knowledge left her incensed.

"From where I was standing," she said with a brittle laugh, "your silence spoke volumes."

"Please, let me in. Let me explain."

Yes. And maybe with you here, in my arms, I can show you how good we'd be together. How perfect our lives would be in every detail.

Granted, logistically things might be rough at first with her business back in Little Rock, but they'd— She slid her fingers into the hair at her temples and pulled.

Listen to her. Was she stark, raving mad?

This, too, shall pass.

Across the room, Cassie's gaze settled on one of the quotes Noah's mother had needlepointed onto a pillow. Words of wisdom from beyond the grave?

Was the message just that simple? Get over him? Get on with her life?

The man didn't want her, yet here she was, still spinning fairy tales of the two of them magically ending up together. How many times did she have to be reminded that for her at least, there was no such thing as fairy tales—only cold, hard reality.

Throwing open her closet, she tugged off the nightgown she'd hoped to wear again on her wedding night. She'd been so excited dashing off to Olivetti's dress shop yesterday to buy it while Evelyn had once again stayed with the babies. The pink floral was a radical departure from her usual black or elegant ivory. It'd made her feel as pretty on the outside as thinking about being Noah's wife had made her feel on the inside.

Swallowing back still more tears, she savagely reached for one of her standard severe black dresses.

"Cass," Noah said. "Look, I know right about now you must be hating me, and I don't blame you. But—"

"Stop. Please don't feel you have to bother with explanations." *Especially since only a few minutes earlier, I felt like I knew you better than myself.* "Kelsey—not to mention Tiffany, and all of the other members of the support group already warned me you weren't the marrying type. I was just too naive to listen." *Too sure that what you and I shared was so special that for me, you'd break your long-standing rule.*

"I'm sorry," he said.

Me, too.

"THANK YOU," Cassie said to Noah two hours later, hair arranged in a severe French twist, eyes shaded from the brutal sun by dark designer sunglasses, confidence boosted by full makeup, black silk stockings, black dress and black patent pumps.

The babies were already fastened in their safety seats in the long black limo she'd paid extra to have rushed from Fayetteville. Star-for-a-Day Limo Service had also agreed to send someone to transport her car later that afternoon. But looking at it now, knowing it would only remind her of her time spent with Noah, she reached into her purse for the keys.

"Here," she said, handing them to Noah.

"Right. Guess the guy coming to pick her up is gonna need these."

Swallowing back tears, knowing herself unable to speak, she shook her head.

"What? You want me to drive it down to Little Rock?"

"No. Give it to Jimmy."

"For him to drive?"

Again, all she could do was shake her head.

"You're not making sense."

"Give the car to Jimmy—for keeps."

"Let me get this straight. You're giving a forty-thousand dollar ride to Jimmy?"

She nodded. It'd be worth a million dollars to her to be rid of the painful reminder of the beautiful time they'd shared.

"Whatever," he said, lips pressed tight, muscle popping in his jaw while he pocketed the keys. "Give me a call, though, if you reconsider."

"I won't. Please tell him I'll have my attorney sign over the title."

He nodded, and with the limo's smooth engine purring behind them, tainting the air with the slight smell of exhaust, they both worked hard to look anywhere but at each other.

Obert Undem stood in his driveway, fiddling with his mower.

Mrs. Kleghorn was watering her marigolds.

Mr. and Mrs. Dickenson were out walking Artie.

As busy as they all seemed to be, they still had plenty of time left for shooting curious glances her and Noah's way.

Cassie bit her lower lip to keep from crying.

It was hard enough leaving Noah, but she was also leaving Brenda and her delicious burgers. Ernie and his snakes. Evelyn and Kelsey and—aw, who was she kidding? She'd grown to love this whole kooky town as much as this man.

As the sun beat mercilessly on her all-black ensemble, Cassie cursed the heavens for not postponing the previous afternoon's cooling rain until today.

But then, please. Nothing else in her life was going right. Why should the weather?

"I wish you would reconsider this whole limo bit,"

Noah finally said. "At least stay the night. I'll drive you home in the morning."

She shook her head, held out her hand for him to shake.

"Whatever," he said, clasping her hand, only not shaking it, but kissing it. "You have to know I never meant to hurt you."

"I know." But the knowing didn't make it hurt any less.

"Okay, then," he said, muscle still popping in his jaw. "Guess this is it then. Have a safe trip."

Because it would have hurt too bad to carry on this sham of a conversation for even one minute longer, Cassie just nodded before settling into the back seat between the girls.

Noah slammed the door, then patted the top of the roof, signaling the driver to go.

Cassie held on to her tears until seeing the sign saying that they'd left Riverdale's city limits. Then, and only then, did she let her misery flow.

She'd known better than to open her heart to another man. Hadn't she learned anything from what Tom had done?

Only this time was even worse, because things didn't have to turn out this way. If only she had left yesterday as planned, at the very least, she could have had Noah in her life, and the girls' lives, as a friend for many years to come.

True, but wouldn't that have ultimately hurt even worse?

Knowing she loved him, having to see him, pretending the whole time that she felt nothing more for him than friendship? *That* would have hurt much worse.

This way, the cut had been clean. Initially agonizing, but over.

Now, all that was left to do was let the healing begin.

"GREAT PARTY, NOAH!" Jimmy waved his barbecued chicken leg before chomping down.

Noah stood at his grill scowling.

Unbelievable. Two weeks after Cass and the babies had left, and he was still creeped out by the quiet that'd descended over his house. So much so that he'd had to go and throw this party. An idea that had seemed good at the time, but now he was wondering if he'd gone overboard with the guest list.

The loud-mouthed gang of off-duty deputies and the fire department guys—currently engrossed in a death match volleyball game with a couple of emergency room doctors and the high school football and basketball coaches—apparently thought the crowd was just right.

Van Halen blared from the boom box Noah had set up outside for the occasion.

Mrs. Kleghorn glared from her backyard petunia bed.

"…so then, Kristen looked up at me and said, 'Daddy, you make the best cereal in the whole wide world.'" While the guys seated in lawn chairs around Ian Deaver carried on about how cute his latest kid story was, then started in with telling their own, Noah suppressed the craziest urge to jump right in with one of his own stories. How Noelle had spit up on him that Sunday afternoon at the grill. Or how cute Cass and his girls had looked curled up in his bed.

Trouble was, they weren't *his* girls.

Never would be.

Could've been, but he'd turned their mother down— a good thing, seeing how much more fun he was having with the guys.

Noah's dad wandered up. "How you been?"

"I'm all right. Finally caught up on my sleep now that Zane seems to have left town."

"Plus, I'd imagine it was a relief getting your house back to yourself."

"Oh sure. Heck, yeah. You know how rough it is having a baby around and all—try multiplying that by two."

His dad sagely nodded.

"How've you been? Heard you been dating a certain pretty blonde from Harrison." Noah winked, giving his old man a guy-to-guy shoulder nudge.

"Damn, this town's gossip chain is efficient. Her name's Marcia. Real cute and bubbly. Not half as pretty as your mother, but then nobody ever quite measures up to your first love. Marcia's as much as admitted to feeling the same about her husband, Cal."

"I take it he died?"

Noah's dad nodded.

"I don't mean to get in your business," Noah said, "but it surprises me to hear you so melancholy about

Mom. I mean, when she was alive, you two could hardly stand being in the same room.''

"True." Misty-eyed, his old man took a swig of his beer. "I guess after a while, I got tired of her cold shoulder. Tired of trying. But that doesn't mean I ever got tired of looking at her. Loving her.''

Embarrassed by his dad's sudden show of emotion, no doubt brought on by one too many Bud Lights, Noah said, "Yeah, well, women. What're you going to do?''

Nodding, his dad said, "She ever tell you she was married to a guy before me?''

Noah was so shocked by this bit of news that he accidentally snapped a hot dog in half with his tongs. He tossed the broken halves to Ian's golden lab who'd been contentedly lying in wait beside the deck, no doubt hoping for just such a windfall to come zinging his way.

"Richard was her high school sweetheart. They got married summer after graduation, then he got called up for Vietnam. Died his first tour. Year later, she moved to Riverdale, hoping for a fresh start. Back then, Grandpa Clyde owned a shoe store on Cherry Street. Forget the name. Anyway, I was smitten from the first time I saw her—kind of like you were with Cass.''

Noah focused on the grill, squeezing his eyes briefly shut. Guess that town gossip chain worked both ways.

"Lord, but your momma was something back then. Hair so blond, you'd think you were lookin' at the sun.''

Noah had loved his mom, but it was another woman he saw. A woman with hair that glinted fire in the sun.

''We casually dated, but the only time I ever remember seeing your mom truly happy aside from later, when she was playing with you, was when she talked about Richard and the way things used to be with him. I tried making her happy...'' He gazed across the crowded lawn as if no one were there save for her. ''Tried so damned hard, but never could. I like this Marcia, son. Real well. Both of us have our closets full of ghosts, but...'' As his words trailed off, he shrugged.

And again, Noah's mind wandered to the parallel between his ghosts and Cass's. Like his mom, she'd been married before, but unlike his mom, she now despised her former spouse.

''You thinking of marrying her—Marcia?'' Noah asked.

''Maybe.'' His dad winked. ''But first hand me one of those dogs.''

ON A RAINY Monday morning, three weeks after she'd said goodbye to the only man she feared she might ever truly love, Cassie stepped off of the elevators leading to her firm, babies in tow.

''Good morning, Ginnie,'' she said to her receptionist, forcing a bright tone.

''Cassie!'' The young, pretty brunette dashed out from behind her antique cherry desk, crushing her boss in a hug before turning her attention to the babies.

"They're beautiful! We were all hoping you'd come in soon for a visit."

"Sorry it took me so long. Who knew sleep deprivation could be this rough?" Cassie crossed her fingers against her half truth. Oh, it was true enough that she was sleep-deprived, but had she been sleepy with Noah, she'd have still felt radiant, while without him, she just felt like a big tired blob.

The worst part of her depression was that she knew better. She was a strong, capable, independent woman who, even while she'd been married, had never been this emotionally bonded to a man. She'd loved Tom, but she'd never felt this all-consuming need for him. Like just being with Noah was a vitamin her body badly craved.

"Oh, I'm sure caring for these two is a full-time job," Ginnie said with a sympathetic smile. "Which one is this?" she asked, picking up a baby.

"Noelle."

"Ah, so this is the one named after the hunk who saved you. Chloe told us all about your whirlwind romance."

Chloe has as big of a mouth as Brenda!

"So? Do you think he'll pop the question?"

"No," Cassie said, picking up Hope's carrier, then striding toward her office, black pumps echoing off the Italian marble floor. "Our relationship wasn't like that. We were just friends."

"Sure," Ginnie said, hustling after her. "I understand."

Opening the double doors leading to her office, for

the first time since returning to Little Rock to the starkly modern house she'd shared with Tom, Cassie felt at home. Calmed by cloth-covered ivory walls, gauzy ivory sheers framing a tenth-floor view of the Arkansas River and North Little Rock, and beyond that, rolling green hills dotted with homes and businesses.

Aside from the view, her mahogany desk and a few other assorted antiques and pictures, everything else in the room was pale ivory from the carpet to the plush furniture. She'd planned it that way to showcase the view of the vibrant city she loved.

Only standing with her palms pressed to the cool glass, she squeezed her eyes closed, not seeing Little Rock, but Riverdale. And the back of Noah's Suburban where she'd fought to bring her children safely into the world. The hospital room with its fragrant bouquets. The cozy little house where she'd once again learned to laugh and live and love.

She saw all the things she'd wanted to change. The courtyard at the sheriff's station she'd dreamed of one day filling with bright, fragrant flowers and hope. The fences she'd wanted to mend with Brenda. The two of them had somehow gotten off on the wrong foot, but given time, they could have shared jokes over Tater Tots, burgers and Brenda's fabulous malts.

And Noah…given more time, maybe even things with him could have been different. Better.

Forever.

"All your personal mail is in the basket on your desk, along with your phone messages," Ginnie said.

"But I'm sure you don't feel like going through all of it today."

"No, I think I will," Cassie said, taking Hope from her carrier, then easing into her buttery-soft ivory leather desk chair. "What do you think, sweetie? Ready to jump right into the family business?" *While Mommy pretends everything is just great when in actuality, everything but you and your sister is wrong?*

"NEVER MIND where you've been. What's this?" Noah asked Zane well after midnight on a Friday night, dust from the dirt road that cut through Floyd's largest pasture swirling eerily in his Blazer's headlights. On the back seat floorboard of the kid's beat-up Dodge Dart, he'd found a half-dozen empty beer cans, but what really made Noah's day was the glass tube he was now holding up. When the kid didn't answer, Noah smacked his hand against the car's trunk. "What is this?"

"What's it look like?" Zane said, eyes darting and wild. Probably still high. "Haven't you ever seen a bong?"

"That's it," Noah said, tired and cranky, and in no mood to put up with one more second of this kid's crap. "Time for you and me to have a nice long talk with a breathalyzer." Slapping the kid into cuffs, he escorted him to the Blazer and got out his kit.

"I'm not doing that test," Zane said. "I didn't do a damned thing wrong."

"Fine. Let's talk about it more down at the station."

"I've got rights, you know."

"You sure do, and seeing how you've just been caught with all manner of illegal goodies in your car, not to mention the fact that there's still that little matter of the liquor store robbery hanging over your head, you get to hear all about my rights to take you to court."

BACK AT THE STATION, Noah had Jimmy check Zane into Riverdale's finest barred-window motel where he'd have a premium view of a lovely concrete block wall.

Hours later, seated behind his desk, forehead resting in his hands, Noah didn't even look up when a knock sounded on his door. "Yeah?"

"Sheriff?" Jimmy asked, helping himself to one of the guest chairs that had finally been cleared now that Noah spent every waking moment at work.

"What's up?" he said, glancing the deputy's way.

"Got something you might want to hear."

"So? Out with it."

"You know those prints you had us take off the bottles at Floyd's?"

"Yeah."

"And the liquor store?"

"Yeah?"

"And even the green tractor tires, footprints and the green mayor's statue?"

"Lord, Jimmy, would you please get to your point."

"Something's wrong with 'em."

"You mean they're not clear enough to be conclusive?"

"No," Jimmy said. "I mean none of them match

up with Zane's. And the drug paraphernalia we just found in his car, and all those beer cans. His prints aren't on any of those, either. And Briggs just watched that liquor store video again, and there's no way either of those boys was Zane.''

''Oh, come on. Had to be.''

''No, sir. Zane's hair's a good four or five inches longer than either of the boys' hair on that tape.''

A sickening heat flooded Noah's chest. ''Crap.''

''And Sheriff? There's one more thing.''

Great. ''What's that?''

''Zane. He's in his cell bawling like a baby. Me and Briggs never seen anything like it.''

Sighing, Noah made his way to the kid's cell and let himself in. ''Mind telling me what's going on?'' he asked.

''Nothing.'' Zane sat huddled in the cell's far corner, hugging his knees.

''Then why you crying?''

''What do you care? No matter what I say, you already know I'm guilty.''

Noah shrugged.

''I hate it when you do that. All the kids at school hate it, too. Like when you come give us all those self-righteous *Don't Do Drugs* speeches, and then when someone asks you the really tough questions, you just turn all red and shrug. It's lame.''

Thanks. My ego really needed all that on top of what I'm already going through with Cass. ''Great. Anything else I need to know?''

''Yeah, that I know you've got your heart set on

saving me, but that I don't need your help. I'm going to make something of myself without help from you or my dad or anyone else. Maybe sign up for the marines. Or get a scholarship to that welding school they advertise for over in Tulsa.''

"Good, Zane. Both of those sound like real good choices.''

"*My* choices. I don't know who died and left you thinking you're all in charge, but you're not—least not of me. Hell, you can't even get your own life straight. I don't know what gives you the right to go preaching to everybody else about how they live theirs.''

"Really a big fan of mine, are you, Zane?''

"Number Eight. Ring a bell?''

Noah shook his head.

"Paula Hinkle. She's my girlfriend's sister, and you did her wrong.''

Hardening his jaw, Noah said, "I'm not having this conversation with you.''

"She said you played house with her. Acted all like you were going to marry her, then turned cold fish so she'd send you packing. Real class act there, Sheriff.''

"Stow it, Zane.''

"Or what? You gonna arrest me again for telling the truth? Like how everyone in town is talking about this latest chick of yours you ran off?''

"Enough.'' Fists clenched, on his feet, Noah said, "I'll run by your place on my way home. See if I can round up your dad.''

"Don't do me any favors. Oh, and by the way, seeing how you don't seem capable of solving any crimes yourself, I'll give you a clue—I'm not your man who keeps messing with old Floyd, and I didn't rob that liquor store. But I know who did.''

''And…''

Zane laughed. ''You just expect me to give them up? I've seen all the cop shows. I don't spill a damned thing without signed immunity from all of your bogus charges.''

Noah closed his eyes and sighed. Raked his fingers through his hair. It was going to be another long night.

Chapter Sixteen

Just before dawn, Noah fell into his bed, hugging the one pillow that still smelled of Cass's exotic shampoo. Just breathing in her fragrance eased the tightness in his chest.

How could he have been so wrong about Zane?

Wrong about Zane?

Ha! Try wrong about *everything!*

His job was a mess. Turned out he had a whole town full of teenaged trouble. Those so-called sweet girls he'd been seeing at the diner and volunteering at the hospital—he'd wished Hope and Noelle would be just like them one day—were the ones messing with Floyd. They'd also stolen Delores's chocolate Santas from the Dollar General sale bin. Zane's older brother, Todd, robbed the liquor store.

Noah hadn't even known Todd was back in town. And it was little wonder Zane had been crying that night Noah had taken him in. When Zane had threatened to turn Todd in for the robbery, Todd and his pal, both high on Lord only knew what, had kept him tied up for days, feeding him nothing but doughnuts and

Mountain Dew. The night Noah picked up Zane, he'd finally made a break for it when Todd had passed out close enough to him that he'd managed to swipe his pocket knife and keys.

What kind of a sheriff was he? To have let a kidnapping go on right under his nose? To have been fooled by those girls' innocent appearances.

Turns out the shoplifting, vandalizing trio had moved into that swanky new subdivision south of town. Their daddies were executives for one of the state's largest companies. With dads always at work, and moms either working themselves or keeping busy with charities, the girls had pretty much been running wild.

All along, Zane had been the one staying home nights doing homework. The green on his fingers? Dye from a school science experiment.

So what kind of sheriff did that make Noah? Lousy.

Lousy also seemed to sum up how he was doing with his personal life.

All he wanted was about a week's sleep, but he couldn't even get that because every time he closed his eyes he saw *her*. Piercing him with that haunting jade-green stare. What did she want from him? What did he want from himself?

I want to be with her and the girls. Not just for a week or two, but forever. I want to trust that she wants this, too, but how can I be sure she won't just end up dumping me like Darla?

Tossing in the bed, he punched the pillow that didn't smell like Cass.

Maybe Helen had been right, and he was the problem. Maybe all these years he'd been stringing women along, just playing at the fringes of relationships instead of actually being a part of them.

Trouble was, just like in his job where half the time there were no sure bets, no black and white, right or wrong, relationships were the same damned way. Where Cass and Hope and Noelle were concerned, did he love them enough to open himself up to the risk of once again falling?

Or maybe the even bigger question was, if Cass really did love him as much as she claimed, did he open himself up to the risk of flying? If he was going to live happily ever after, he'd have to admit he'd been wrong about Cass.

Tossing again, this time breathing her scent, he dragged her in—at least his memory of her.

Those luminous eyes. That fiery red hair glinting in the sun. Those lips, melting against his with an urgency that even now, weeks later, awakened a hunger in him.

But then there were the girls.

Shoot, Noah thought he'd been ready to be a father, but if any of what Zane had said was true, he obviously didn't know the first thing about being a good dad.

And those delinquent girls. They were a product of what society generally considered well above average families, yet even with two loving parents and no shortage of material extras, somewhere along the line, those girls had taken a wrong turn.

How could he have missed that? How could he ever

learn to be an effective dad when he wasn't even an effective sheriff?

One day at a time.

Yesterday afternoon, he'd finally found the courage to enter Cass and the babies' room only to be hit across his forehead with a two-by-four of guilt.

Dust.

Brown-leafed plants.

Achingly familiar scents of Oriental perfume and baby lotion.

Those damned quotes on his mother's pillows that never had made any sense. Shoot, if she'd spent half as much time on her marriage as she had stitching those pillows, she and Noah's dad might've had a chance.

Disgusted with himself, and his life, Noah had just turned to leave when one quote had caught his eye.

One day at a time.

"You trying to tell me something, Momma?" he asked.

Strangely enough, just the asking made his heart lighter. Could life truly be that simple? Little more than a matter of tackling problems one day at a time? One minute at a time?

If that truly were the case, why hadn't his mom seen it? Or maybe she had, but by then it'd been too late to reverse a lifetime's sorrow.

But for him and Cass…

Maybe he wasn't too late, but just in the nick of time.

Maybe once they worked through their own issues,

they could learn to be parents together. And maybe one day, next year, or the year after that, they could have kids of their own—not that the girls wouldn't be his once he adopted them, but—

Aw, hell, what was he doing still lying here in bed when he could be on his way to Little Rock?

"Ah, Cass…" Ginnie fiddled with her pearl necklace. "You might wanna come see someone."

Cassie looked up from the pile of marble, fabric and paint samples she'd been playing with on her floor. "No, sweetie," she said when Hope put a strip of ruby-colored suede to her lips. "What's up? Did the Andersons finally get back from Greece?"

"No such luck."

"That Indian silk finally get here?"

Ginnie worried her lower lip. "No luck on that, either."

"Don't keep me in suspense. Geesh, from the look on your face, I'd guess the FBI was out in the reception area." Dressed in a loose, bright cotton animal print jumper, Cassie grappled to her feet, taking Hope along with her.

Noelle was still in her portable crib indulging in a midmorning nap.

"Well, it's sort of something like the FBI."

Cassie's blood ran cold. "What do you mean, sort of?" Could this have something to do with Tom? Was her nightmare where he was concerned still not over? Wasn't she already going through enough in losing

Noah? Did she really have to go through another bout of ancient angst history?

"Well… First, all these strange deliveries started showing up. I knew you were busy with the Bingham presentation, so I didn't want to bother you, but there was this carton of diapers, and then boxes and boxes of baby toys and clothes and hats."

"Get back to the FBI part," Cassie said, heart pounding. "Is this person a man or woman? What do they look like?"

"Me," Noah said, strolling through her office door, dressed in his rumpled uniform with two mammoth, stuffed pink hippos tucked under each arm. "I thought the girls could use a little fattening up."

Instead of laughing, as the insensitive lout no doubt must've thought she'd do at his lame joke, she tucked Hope beside her sister in the portable crib.

"That was funny," Noah said. "Get it? Fatten up? Hippos?" He wagged one of the adorable pink toys.

"Ginnie, would you mind leaving us alone?"

Her receptionist cast Noah a stare every bit as nosy as ones from her labor and delivery ward nurse or Mrs. Kleghorn, then looked back to Cassie and behind her hand mouthed, "He the one?"

Cass barely nodded.

Ginnie beamed, then hustled back to her desk, shutting the door behind her.

"My reputation precedes me, huh?" Noah asked, helping himself to one of the Oreos Cassie had on her desk.

"What are you doing here?" she asked, not in the

mood for anything less than a full-on, bended knee proposal—the kind she knew full well he had no intention of ever giving any woman, let alone her!

"We have some unfinished business."

"Says who?"

"Me, me!" Noah said, dumping one hippo on her guest chair, then holding the other in front of his mouth to "speak."

"That's real mature," she said. *Almost as mature as your inability, or unwillingness, to commit to a marriage we both know could be terrific, only you're too damned stubborn, too sure you know everything there ever was to know about love, to give yourself—us—a second chance.*

"I'm sorry," the bouncing hippo still covering Noah's incredibly handsome face said. "I didn't mean to make you mad."

"Yeah, well you did." Cassie didn't even try stopping her tears. "You hurt me way worse than Tom, because looking back on it, I never loved Tom the way I loved you. So there, I've let you in on my big secret, now you can go."

"I'm not going anywhere," Noah said, this time his voice his own while pulling her into an awkward hug with the hippo lodged between them.

"Can't you put that thing down?" she asked, pushing him and his insincere embrace away. "So I can tell you to get lost and stay lost with proper enthusiasm."

"I've been out of my mind without you," he said. "You're beautiful."

Thank you. So are you. "Sweet talk and gifts will get you nowhere, Noah. I'm not interested in spending the rest of my life dating. I want a forever kind of commitment or nothing at all."

"Whew," he said, hippo back in front of his face. "Tough crowd."

"Dammit," she said, tears back, angrily swiping them away. "Would you stop kidding around? I'm serious. I want you gone, Noah."

"Even if I've come bearing this?" He wagged the hippo once more, and she swatted the stupid thing away. "How many times do I have to—"

The pig landed with a metallic twang against the square foot marble samples she'd spread across the carpet. Along with that twang, a shiny sparkle of gold had shot off of the bow around the animal's neck, rolling under the sofa.

"Great," Noah said, heading that way. "Just my dumb luck, here I am, finally ready to propose to the woman I love, and I can't even get that right. Maybe I went about this all wrong?"

He winced while going down on his knees in front of the sofa.

"What's wrong?" she asked, sitting beside him on the floor. "Are you hurt?"

"Shoot, yeah. Wasn't your pride banged up when I turned down your proposal?"

"I'm not talking about your pride, but your leg. You're obviously in pain."

He shrugged, looked away.

"Don't do that," she said, hand on his shoulder. "Not now. Not with so much at stake."

"I've got a bum knee, okay?"

"Did you hurt it at work?"

He was again looking away, and there went that muscle in his jaw. "I thought Tiffany and Kelsey filled you in?"

"On what?"

"Darla. My ex-wife."

"They did. They said you both got bored with commitment. What does any of that have to do with us?"

He sharply laughed. "Sounds like something they'd do. Leaving out the juicy parts."

"Okay," she said. "Let's hear 'em."

"Why? You won't believe me."

"Try me."

He stared at her long and hard, took a deep breath before saying, "Until you, Darla was the last woman I ever really trusted."

"Does that mean you trust me now?"

"Honestly, I'm not sure. I guess I've gotten pretty good at hiding my feelings over the years." Taking her hands in hers, he gave them a squeeze. "Just like I've hidden the way I feel about you—really, good— I hide the way I feel about a lot of other things, too. Not so good things. Like my parents and a lot of the crap that goes down at work and my bum knee."

"How did you hurt it?"

He started to shrug, then stopped himself with a sheepish grin. "Sorry. Guess old habits die hard."

"That's all right," she said, hand to his cheek. "Carry on."

"Anyway, I didn't hurt it doing anything glamorous like movie stunts or anything. Just flew up to catch a Hail Mary pass and came down wrong. Busted it five ways to Sunday."

"When? Just out playing ball with the guys?"

"You might say that," he said with another grin. "The guys and about sixty-thousand screaming Hog fans."

Hands over her mouth, Cassie's eyes widened. "You're *that* Noah Wheeler?"

He beamed. "In the flesh."

"Oh, my gosh. You were like a legend. I always wondered what happened to you."

"Yeah, well, now you know. Once Darla found out the scouts were no longer interested in me, she pretty much moved on to greener pastures while I…"

"Came home," Cassie said when he seemed to have trouble finding his own words. "Where instead of sitting around feeling sorry for yourself, you've worked yourself silly trying to help everyone under the sun."

"Don't make me out to be some kind of hero, Cass. I'm just an ordinary guy, doing my best, and most days failing."

Up on her knees, cupping both of his cheeks now to draw him into the sweetest of kisses, she said, "Don't you ever call yourself an ordinary guy again, Noah Wheeler."

"Why? It's the truth."

Swallowing back tears, she shook her head. "You

will forever be my hero. Hero to my girls. Hero to my very soul. I love you. I love you so much it hurts. And I sometimes just want to—''

''Shh…'' he said, on his knees, too, silencing her with a long, lingering kiss. ''Marry me, Cass. Make me whole. Make me—''

Cassie tackled him mid-sentence, pressing him to the floor, landing herself atop him where she kissed his forehead, eyebrows and nose. Cheeks, chin and ultimately his lips. Those, wonderful, fabulous delicious lips.

''Whoa… Wait a minute,'' he said, sliding his fingers into her hair. ''We can't do this yet. I still have to formally propose. And I can't very well do that without a ring.''

''Forget the ring,'' she said, ''Tell me why you had this turn-around from being so dead set against marriage to now being so gung ho for it?''

''Do I have to? I mean, all that stuff's kind of touchy-feely for a guy like me. It was bad enough thinking it. I don't wanna say it.''

''Tell me,'' she said, silencing his protests with another kiss.

Sitting beside her on the sofa, he did tell her everything not only in his mind, but his heart. He told her about the mistake he'd made with Zane, and how that had led him to question many of his other long-time beliefs, like why his parents' marriage hadn't worked out. ''Their not getting along had nothing to do with me,'' he said. ''But with Mom being incapable of letting go of her first love. When I think of how much my dad adored her, and how much she gave up by not giving him a chance… I don't know, maybe as a kid, being helpless to fix their marriage flipped a switch in me that made me that much more determined to fix everything else. But this whole mess with Zane, and you—they made me see that there are some things I just can't fix. No matter how hard I try. Those are the things I have to surrender to a higher power. As for my busted heart… That, I'm entrusting to you.''

''Oh, Noah,'' she said, cupping his cheek, brushing a stray tear with the pad of her thumb. ''Stop. You've told me enough.'' *I can't bear seeing you in any more pain.*

''No. I still haven't told you how much I love you.''

''I know. I love you, too.''

''Yeah, well, you still need a formal proposal, too—with a proper ring.''

''Okay, then, looks like there's only one thing we can do….''

In unison, the shoved and tugged the massive antique sofa back from the wall.

OUT IN THE reception area, Ginnie's eyes widened.

What was going on in there?

If only Evelyn and Kelsey were here. They'd know what to do. Ever since their shopping trip to Little Rock—the trip Ginnie and Chloe suspected had been more about checking up on Cassie than buying clothes, they'd all become fast friends. Ginnie now gave them regular updates on Cassie's usually despondent mood.

"Now what're they doing?" Chloe asked, balanced on the arm of one of the reception area chairs.

"Beats me." Ginnie pressed her ear tighter to Cassie's closed office door. "All I hear is a lot of grunting and banging on—oh, wait. I think that was a giggle."

"Hmm… Giggles and grunting. Always an excellent sign," Chloe said with a satisfied smile. "Sounds to me as if our favorite couple finally figured out how to make up."

Ginnie's eyes widened as her cheeks reddened. "Then all that banging in there is…"

Chloe, wearing the calm expression of one who was a self-proclaimed expert in such matters, wisely nodded.

Ginnie gave her a high five. "You're bad."

"Yep. And Cassie finding the man of her dreams is oh-so-good. Let's give Kelsey and Evelyn the great news."

"Oh—and they can call Tiffany."

"And she can call Nurse Helen."

"And she can call…"

Epilogue

"Daddy? Are we almost home?" Five-year-old Noelle had her nose to the Suburban's rear window while her sister played an electronic Disney game.

"Just about, pumpkin."

Cass was sound asleep, with her head and neck scrunched in what looked to Noah like a damned uncomfortable position.

He pressed his foot harder on the gas pedal.

They'd been spending a long weekend in Branson when Cass had told him she felt like she might be having contractions. Judging by his last experience with delivering babies, Noah had been all for driving her straight to the hospital nearest Silver Dollar City.

But, oh no, Cass being Cass, she wanted to have their son in Riverdale. She'd already had babies out of town once, she'd told him with a sassy wink. Never again.

And so, fool for love that he was, he'd bundled her and the whining girls into the truck and here they were, still a good thirty minutes from home, but so far so good.

"Noah?" Cass said a little while later, voice groggy from he hoped sleep and not pain.

"Yeah?"

"Did the girls spill juice in the back seat?"

"No." On a straight stretch, he glanced her way. "Why?"

"My feet are—" She flew her hands to her mouth. "Oh no...not again?"

"What, sweetie? What?"

"My water broke."

"Here? In the truck? You've got to be kidding."

Flashing him a grin, she said, "Gotcha!"

"Grr." He tightened his grip on the wheel. "Woman, you make me crazy."

"Good," she said with another wink. "I love you."

"I love you, too. Lord only knows why."

"Let's see... Because I'm ravishing and gorgeous and can eat you under the table any day in a Tater Tot battle at Brenda's..."

"All true."

"And because I give good back rubs and—ouch."

He rolled his eyes. "Oh please, you expect me to fall for that again?"

"No, really. This time I'm not joking."

"You are such a bad fibber. I swear, once we get my son safely out of you, as the newly reelected law around these parts, I'm turning you over to Deputy Zane."

"Ooh, big threat there," she said, faking a show of concern. "He's turned into such a teddy bear since marrying Heidi, it's a wonder he arrests anyone."

"Hey, you have to admit, he's doing a great job with the high school crowd. He really relates."

"True, and—ouch. Noah, I'm really not kidding. Something's going on down there. Think maybe you should pull over?"

"What I think is that if these girls weren't in the back, I'd pull over all right, and toss you over my knee for messing with me."

"Mmm," she teased. "You know how I like it rough."

"You're incorrigible, Mrs. Wheeler."

"Thank you, Mr. Wheeler."

"Give it to me straight, babe. You really hurting?"

She winced again. "Let's put it this way—just in case, how about less chitchat and more driving?"

Determined never again to have this wonderful woman's life, along with the life of one of their children quite literally in his hands, Noah gave the truck's engine more gas, and his wife's belly a gentle pat.

* * * * *

Watch for Laura Marie Altom's
next American Romance,
SANTA BABY,
coming in November!

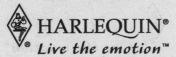

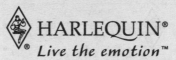

If you enjoyed what you just read,
then we've got an offer you can't resist!

Take 2 bestselling love stories FREE!

Plus get a FREE surprise gift!

Clip this page and mail it to Harlequin Reader Service®

IN U.S.A.	IN CANADA
3010 Walden Ave.	P.O. Box 609
P.O. Box 1867	Fort Erie, Ontario
Buffalo, N.Y. 14240-1867	L2A 5X3

YES! Please send me 2 free Harlequin American Romance® novels and my free surprise gift. After receiving them, if I don't wish to receive anymore, I can return the shipping statement marked cancel. If I don't cancel, I will receive 4 brand-new novels every month, before they're available in stores! In the U.S.A., bill me at the bargain price of $4.24 plus 25¢ shipping & handling per book and applicable sales tax, if any*. In Canada, bill me at the bargain price of $4.99 plus 25¢ shipping & handling per book and applicable taxes**. That's the complete price and a savings of at least 10% off the cover prices—what a great deal! I understand that accepting the 2 free books and gift places me under no obligation ever to buy any books. I can always return a shipment and cancel at any time. Even if I never buy another book from Harlequin, the 2 free books and gift are mine to keep forever.

154 HDN DZ7S
354 HDN DZ7T

Name _____ (PLEASE PRINT)

Address _____ Apt.#

City _____ State/Prov. _____ Zip/Postal Code

* Terms and prices subject to change without notice. Sales tax applicable in N.Y.
** Canadian residents will be charged applicable provincial taxes and GST.
All orders subject to approval. Offer limited to one per household and not valid to current Harlequin American Romance® subscribers.
® are registered trademarks owned and used by the trademark owner and or its licensee.

AMER04   ©2004 Harlequin Enterprises Limited

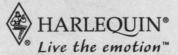